KU-503-352

Cathy Hopkins

Truth,
Dare, Kiss,
Promise

Double Dare

Piccadilly Press • London

Thanks to Brenda Gardner, Yasemin Uçar, Jon Appleton,
Melissa Patey and the rest of the team of fabsters at Piccadilly.
To Rosemary Bromley at Juvenilia. To Steve Lovering for his constant sup-
port and help on all aspects of the book and for going out and to turn on
the heating on in my office/shed on wintry days so that it's not freezing
when I get out there. And to a dear male friend who provided so many
great dating disaster stories for this book but who shalll remain anonymous
so that his street cred remains intact. (You know who you are . . .)

First published in Great Britain in 2005
by Piccadilly Press Ltd,
5 Castle Road, London NW1 8PR

This edition published 2008

Text copyright © Cathy Hopkins, 2005

All rights reserved. No part of this publication may be reproduced,
stored in a retrieval system, or transmitted in any form or by any
means, electronic, mechanical, photocopying, recording or
otherwise, without the prior permission of the copyright owner.

The right of Cathy Hopkins to be identified as Author of this work
has been asserted by her in accordance with the
Copyright, Designs and Patents Act 1988

A catalogue record for this book is available from
the British Library

ISBN: 978 1 85340 971 4 (paperback)

1 3 5 7 9 10 8 6 4 2

Printed in the UK by CPI Bookmarque, Croydon, CR0 4TD
Typeset by M Rules, London
Set in Garamond and Fineprint
Cover design by Simon Davis
Cover illustration by Susan Hellard

Mixed Sources
Product group from well-managed
forests and other controlled sources
www.fsc.org Cert no. TT-COC-002227
© 1996 Forest Stewardship Council
FSC

Truth,
Dare, Kiss,
Promise

Double Dare

52 392 993 0

Cathy Hopkins lives in London with her husband and two cats, Emmylou and Otis. The cats appear to be slightly insane. Their favourite game is to run from one side of the house to the other as fast as possible, then see if they can fly if they leap high enough off the furniture. This is usually at three o'clock in the morning and they land on anyone who happens to be asleep at the time.

Cathy spends most of her time locked in a shed at the bottom of the garden pretending to write books but is actually in there listening to music, hippie dancing and checking her Facebook page.

Apart from that, Cathy has joined the gym and spends more time than is good for her making up excuses as to why she hasn't got time to go.

The TRUTH, DARE, KISS, PROMISE series

Find out more at www.piccadillypress.co.uk
Join Cathy's Club at www.cathyhopkins.com

D Day

'WHAT EXACTLY DO BOYS WANT?' asked Cat as we sat on the bus on the way to school on the first day back after the Easter holidays. 'I wish I could get into a boy's head for just twenty-four hours and see what goes on in there.'

'You wouldn't find a lot,' said Squidge, laughing. 'Not in Mac's head anyway,'

I punched him. 'Oi! Watch it, mate. You don't know what goes on in here.'

Squidge laughed again. 'The state of the environment, why are we here? Is there a God? I don't think so. More like: see girl, good, mmm, hubba hubba. Want grub, soon. Tired, me sleep through maths class. Ug.'

'And I call you a mate!' I said. 'You don't appreciate my hidden depths.'

'OK,' said Cat. 'So tell me. What were you thinking just

then when you were staring out the window? What deep thoughts were going through that head of yours?'

I'm not a blusher normally but I felt myself go red. She'd caught me out. Today was the day I was dreading with a capital D. It was the day I was going to finish with Becca, and I was going over my goodbye speech for the fifteen millionth thousandth time.

'Oh . . . you know, just thinking about what tortuous horrors lie ahead at school today.'

'Hmm, exactly what I was trying not to think about,' said Cat. 'Think I'll go and talk to Moira at the back. See what she's been up to over the Easter holidays.'

'So much for my magnetic hold over women,' I said when she'd gone. 'Two minutes with me and they can't wait to get away.'

'At least you have Becca,' said Squidge. 'She doesn't seem in any hurry to get away from you. It was like you were joined at the hip over the holidays.'

'Tell me about it,' I said. 'I've already had two text messages from her this morning. But . . . listen, mate, strictly between me and you?'

'Yeah.'

'Just . . . Difficult, this. I like Becca and all, who wouldn't? She's a top babe but . . .'

'You've been thinking about finishing with her?'

'How did you know?'

'D'oh! I'm not stupid. Remember on the film set? You said something about wanting to try a whole bowl of fruit and not just settle for an apple, or something poetic like that.'

I nodded. In the Easter holidays, a film crew had been down filming in Mount Edgecumbe Park. It had been top as half the school had managed to wangle jobs there. Squidge had worked as a runner, Cat and Becca had worked in the catering tent and I'd worked there a few days washing cars. It was a brilliant experience and we met loads of great people, especially the make-up girls. Trouble was, Becca watched me like a hawk if ever she saw me chatting to any of them. It was then I began to question whether I wanted to be in a committed relationship and with Becca, it's certainly that. She calls all the shots: decides where we go, when we go, who we see. And she calls or texts about ten times a day. I was beginning to feel suffocated.

'So when are you going to tell her?' asked Squidge.

'Today. Start the summer term with a clean slate.'

'Hmm. Best of luck.'

'Oh come on, Squidge. Give me more than that. I was hoping you could tell me what to say?'

When I first moved down to Cornwall from London just over a year ago, Cat and Squidge had been an item. They'd been going together for ages and Squidge wanted to cut loose and be free to meet other girls. And now he's going with the gorgeous Lia Axford. But he managed to stay friends with Cat. In fact, we're all friends. Me, Squidge, Lia, Cat and Becca. I've hung out with them from the beginning of my time down here and don't want to lose any of them as mates.

'No easy way,' said Squidge. 'Just do it.'

'But *how*? I've already been over the speech a million times. How did you do it with Cat?'

'Ah. I guess I did agonise about it for weeks before . . .'

'Exactly,' I said. 'So don't give me any of that "just do it" crap.'

'But in the end, that's what I had to do. You have to bite the bullet, take the bull by the horns . . .'

'Take the Becca by the horns. Scary. What if she cries?'

Becca is one of those girls who wears her heart on her sleeve and has no problem showing her emotions. And boy, does she have plenty. I didn't want to upset her. I hate scenes. I hate confrontation. I'm like my dad in that way, all for the easy life, and this was going to be difficult. I knew Becca really liked me. A lot. And flattering though it was, I wanted to move on.

As the bus arrived at the school gates, Squidge turned to me and said, 'May the force be with you, Skywalker, my

4

little chum. Just do it and . . . er . . . why are you cowering under the seat?'

I'd ducked down as I'd just seen Becca's dad's VW Polo draw up in front of the bus. Becca was getting out of the back. Am I mad? I asked myself as I peeked up from the floor and watched her walk into school. Dressed all in black today. Black jeans, black strappy top. She's a really good-looking girl. Tall and curvy with long, Titian red hair. She looks like one of the girls in those Pre-Raphaelite paintings by Edward Burne Jones.

'Lost something?' asked Cat as she passed and saw me scrabbling round on the floor.

'Only my mind,' I replied.

'Nothing new there then,' said Cat as she got off the bus and ran to catch Becca up.

Being back at school was horrible. Always is after a break. And it didn't help that we started with double maths followed by chemistry. My favourite subject is art. It's the only thing I'm really any good at. I want to be a cartoonist when I leave school. It's all I've ever wanted to do since I was a kid and although I know I've got a long way to go yet, I hope to develop my own style so that everyone recognises my 'Mac' cartoon when they see one. So I can't see the point of potions, formulas and learning the properties of carbon dioxide.

I spent most of the morning classes going over once again what I was going to say to Becca. She'd texted that she wanted to meet up in the break but I wasn't ready and I'd hidden in the library where I'd decided to try and avoid her for the rest of the morning. Shouldn't be too difficult as she's in Year Nine and I'm in Eleven so we don't do classes together. I'd do it at lunch. No. Bad idea. I might not be able to get her on her own – and how would I do it? I can't exactly land it on her, just as she's munching her sandwiches, like – oh by the way, it's over between us, enjoy your buttie. And I might need more time than we get in the lunch hour, like if she cries and needs me to hug her and talk her through it. No, definitely a bad idea to do it then. If she gets upset then she'd still have to get through the afternoon. No. Can't do that to her. Best do it after school. That way, she can get home and if she's going to cry, she can do it in private. God this stinks. Why don't they teach us important life skills like this in school? A class in how to finish with your girlfriend would be far more useful than learning what the symbols for oxygen and carbon dioxide are. As Mr Daley droned on at the front of the class, I went back to writing my goodbye speech in my head.

I really like you but . . .

Don't take this personally but . . .

It's not that I don't rate you. It's just that I have

discovered that I'm gay and have decided to come out . . .

Actually, Becca, although I'm only sixteen, I have a wife and a kid in London and have been waiting for the right moment to tell you . . .

Actually, Mac died in the Easter holidays and I'm his twin brother from London – and I already have a girlfriend . . .

God appeared in my bedroom last night and told me that I am the Chosen One and must abstain from relationships from now on . . .

Useless, all useless. No. I have to tell the truth. But *how?* Text or e-mail? Something like: CU L8R. MUCH L8R. No, that's the coward's way. I have to do it in person. I owe her that much.

I looked down to see that I had scribbled a cartoon of a boy being hung round the neck from the gallows. Unfortunately, Mr Daley was walking the aisles and had seen my drawing too.

'Ah. Poor lad. Is that how you're feeling today, Macey?' he asked. 'Must be hard for you being back after the holidays.'

I knew the note of concern in his voice was well fake. 'No, sir. I mean yes, sir. I mean . . .'

'You haven't listened to a word I've said in class so far. Have you?'

'Yes, sir. I have.'

'And the properties of carbon dioxide are?'

'Er . . . water . . .'

Mr Daley gave me his scary smile. The scary smile that meant, you are about to be punished. 'This is your GSCE year. No time for messing about. Detention. Lunchtime. Take a slip on the way out.'

'Yes, sir.' I grinned up at him. Excellent, I thought. That gives me a let out from seeing Becca.

Mr Daley gave me a strange look. 'Now, before I go into the properties of sulphur, is anyone else having problems concentrating and would like to join Tom Macey?'

Becca sent me two more text messages while I was in detention saying that she wanted to see me urgently. It's always urgent with her. So I texted back that I'd meet her outside school by the bus stop where she waits for her lift home. That way, we won't have too much time. I can do the dreaded deed. The car will arrive to pick her up, take her home and she won't have to face anyone until she's ready. It was a good plan. Sorted.

All too soon, school was over, I was at the allocated meeting place and Becca was coming out of the gates towards me. She was nearly in front of me, twirling her hair and she looked anxious. I had a moment of panic. Maybe Squidge *had* said something. He might have told Lia what I was planning to do and she might have told Cat and she might have told Becca. No. No, I reassured myself. He wouldn't have. He's my best mate. I could trust him and he knows what those girls are like. Can't keep anything to themselves. What had he said this morning? Just do it? I hitched my school bag further up on my shoulder and took a deep breath.

'Becca . . .'

'Mac,' she said, before I could get any further. 'There's no easy way to say this, so I'm just going to come out with it and be straight. I think we should have a break from one another.'

Woah! That was my line.

'I really, really like you and don't want you to take it personally or anything,' she said as she placed her hand gently on my arm. 'And I want to stay friends. That's really important to me. You're one of the nicest guys I know but I just don't want a boyfriend at the moment.'

Cue a line from me but my vocal cords seemed to have frozen in my throat.

She flicked her hair back and continued with *my* script.

'I just feel that we've become too much of a couple and we need to be a bit more independent . . .'

I was vaguely aware that my goldfish impression needed no more work. I closed my mouth and tried to look casual but everything I'd planned to say had flown out of my brain.

'Er . . . fine . . . right . . .' I finally managed to stammer.

'I am sorry.'

'No. Yeah. Right. It's fine.'

Becca sighed. 'Phew. What a relief that you're taking it like this. I've been in agony all day, dreading this. Are you sure you're OK?'

'I'm fine. Really,' I said although I was anything but. I felt dumbfounded at the way things were turning out. She was dumping *me*! Last thing I expected. It was supposed to be me dumping her, something I thought I'd better let her know right away. 'In fact, I'd been thinking the same thing.'

Becca squeezed my arm. 'Dear Mac,' she said. 'It's so typical of you to say something like that to make it easier for me when I know I must have hurt you. So thanks. I know you'll need some time alone to get your head around this but when you feel ready, we can still be mates, can't we? Hang around with the gang?'

'Yeah. Course.'

'I've been so worried,' she said, then clasped me in a great bear hug. 'You're such a great mate, Mac. I'm so glad this isn't going to spoil things between us.'

She let me go, then scrutinised my face carefully. Probably looking for tears.

'So . . . See you around then.'

'Yeah,' I said. 'See you around.'

It was then that I spied Cat and Lia hovering behind the school gates. They were looking this way and when Cat saw me glance over at them, she darted back out of sight. My humiliation is now total, I thought. Obviously tickets have been sold to the whole school and someone will be around selling binoculars and popcorn any minute.

Becca gave my arm a last squeeze then went back to join Cat and Lia who were still looking on anxiously. Clearly they'd planned the whole scene between them and now were going to go off somewhere and talk over my reaction. I stood there feeling a total idiot. How could I have got it so wrong? I asked myself. I thought she was crazy about me. I must be so seriously rubbish at reading girl's minds.

Girls. Love them. Hate them. I sure don't understand them.

2 Double Dare

ON THE WAY HOME, I got off the bus at the View café up at Whitsand Bay. I didn't feel like facing anyone yet. I wanted time on my own to chill. And compose a letter.

I walked from the bus stop up the slope to the café which is situated on top of the cliff, took a bench at one of the picnic tables outside on the balcony and pulled my notebook out of my school bag.

The café is called the View as it has one of the best views in the area. In the distance to the left you can see the peninsula jutting out at Rame Head and to the right, there are cliffs and unspoilt coastline stretching for as far as the eye can see. It really is stunning. Sea, sky and not much else. The café used to be a greasy spoon type of place serving up endless plates of bacon and eggs to passing ramblers and tourists, but now it's been taken over and has gone more upmarket. That's one of the reasons I like it. It's the only place in the whole area where you can get a decent cappuccino and I've missed them since we left London. Talk about culture shock, I thought as I gazed around me. Just over a year ago, on my way home from school, I'd be sitting on Upper Street in London looking out at the rush hour traffic. Every other building was a café there – Café Rouge, Café Uno, Starbucks, Café Nero – and now, my only option is this isolated place where the only buildings that can be seen are holiday chalets dotted down the cliff and the only customers are the occasional ramblers who happen to be passing by. Still, it's better than nothing.

I miss a lot about London. I miss my mates at my old school. I miss footie on Highbury Fields. Camden Market heaving with people on a Saturday morning. Going to the movies at Screen on the Green, bowling at Finsbury Park, visiting the Tate Modern down on the river, great exhibitions every weekend. It's all so different down here. Beautiful, no doubt, but way quieter. The villages in winter are like ghost towns until the tourists arrive. And who wants to hang out in a ghost town when you're sixteen years old? Not me.

It wasn't exactly part of the plan that we'd end up down here. My sister Jade was doing all right at her school and I was certainly happy in mine. Mum was doing great, running a thriving business as a private caterer for posh people. And Dad worked as a freelance illustrator. We had a large rambling house in Islington, loads of mates round all the time. Happy families.

Then Dad had an affair. Not even a long one. Some girl at one of the studios he worked for. Didn't last but he confessed all to Mum and that was the end of life as we knew it. Mum wanted a divorce and Dad moved out into a small flat while things got sorted.

Within the month, Mum had bundled Jade and me into a car, the removal vans followed and soon we were knocking on Gran's door down here. She has an amazing Victorian house looking over the harbour at Anderton. Wrought iron balconies at the windows, lovely gardens at the front and back. Very picturesque. We used to visit every summer and it was great for a fortnight, then back to London. Grandad died ten years ago and the house is way too big for her on her own, as it has six bedrooms and two receptions. It was beginning to look run down before we got here. I think she's happy enough with the plan as although she's always kept herself busy, she now has company. Mum has made the place look fabulous. It's like an advert out of *Country and Home* magazine. She's even bringing in money from it as we take B&B guests.

I was well pissed off, though, as I wanted to live with

Dad. He's laid-back and easy to live with as opposed to Mum who is a major control freak and for ever organising everyone else's life, as well as her own. But that plan was a no-go as our family home in Islington was soon put on the market. Dad's moved to a semi decent place in Highgate since and when he first went there, I thought, excellent, now's my chance, as there were two bedrooms. Then he got himself a new girlfriend. A new girlfriend with a daughter, Tamara, and she got the spare room. I'm still hoping that I can live there with them, although I haven't broached the subject with Dad yet. That's what the letter is going to be about. Next year I'll be doing A-levels and my plan is to apply to a few sixth-form colleges in London. I'd sleep on the sofa at Dad's or under the dining table, I don't care as long as he lets me live up there where I belong.

'Hey, good drawings,' said the waitress, when she brought me my cappuccino and looked down at my notepad.

'Oh,' I said. 'Thanks.'

As I'd been sitting there thinking about what to write to Dad, I'd been doodling my mates down here. If it hadn't been for them, I'd have gone mental. I'd drawn Squidge looking like a character out of *The Matrix* as he does these days with his dark, spiky hair, long black leather coat and shades. Cat looking like a tabby cat with her short tousled hair and feline face. The stunning Lia, looking like

Botticelli's *Venus* with her long blond hair and willowy figure and Becca looking like Lady Macbeth with a dagger in hand ready to strike. Then me on the end, straw-blond hair, average height and looking stupid with big donkey's ears attached to my head.

'Anyone you know?' said the waitress, smiling as she pointed at the donkey. She was attractive, blonde with pretty green eyes and enormous boobs. I hoped I hadn't been staring at them (the boobs that is, not the eyes).

'Yeah. It's me,' I said. 'Twit of the week.'

'Ah well,' she said. 'It's only Monday.' She had a nice voice: soft, Irish.

I wondered whether I should chat her up as she was definitely giving me the eye. I decided not to risk it as she looked older than me and might only be acting friendly to get a tip. Plus I couldn't trust my feelings regarding girls today. As I'd just learnt from Becca, I couldn't have got it more wrong. Maybe I'd come back another day when I was feeling more confident and check her out again.

'Where've you been?' asked Mum as soon as I walked through the door and into the kitchen. 'Supper's been ready for ages.'

'Nowhere . . . just . . .' I sniffed the air. It smelled wonderful, of cinnamon and baking. 'What you cooking?'

'Carrot cake. Not for you,' she replied as she busied herself taking cakes out of the oven. 'Your dinner is on top of the oven. Probably dried up by now. Oh, and some girl has been phoning. About ten times. When you speak to her, ask her not to call at mealtimes. How was school?'

'What girl?'

'Ask your gran or Jade. They took the calls. Now come and eat,' she said as she piled a plate for me from the pan. I suddenly realised that despite the trauma of the day, I was starving. Pasta in tomato sauce. That'll do me. Although Mum works as a caterer and cooks the most exotic creations for all her clients, she does quick stuff for us. Not that I mind, I wouldn't want to be eating posh nosh with balsamic whatsit every night. Pasta, chips, pizza and sausages. That's what I like. And Mum hasn't done much of her fancy cooking down here. There's no call for it, except sometimes when the Axfords have a do. Now Mum bakes cakes and quiches to sell in Cat's dad's store. And she does breakfast for the B&B guests that we take in. She does it beautifully: freshly baked bread, organic everything, fresh herbs – but I don't think half of them appreciate it. They just want the good old English fry-up in the morning. I think it's a bit of a come down for her as she had a growing reputation up in London and there was even talk of her doing her own recipe book. Still, it was her choice. We could have stayed up there. She could have forgiven Dad, as goodness knows he begged her to in the beginning. Not now, though. He's moved on and I don't blame him. Mum can be scary when you get on her wrong side.

'Aren't you going to phone this girl?' asked Mum when I'd finished supper.

'Nah,' I said. 'Homework to do.' And I retreated upstairs before she got me to do the washing up. It was probably Becca calling in a fit of remorse or worried that I might be upset. Pff to her, I thought. I'd had all the humiliation I could take for one day.

As soon as I got to my room, I put my headphones on, turned the volume up loud and closed my eyes. Nothing like music to obliterate your mind and that's what I needed. Obliteration.

I was just drifting off nicely to a brilliant guitar riff when I felt something crawling up my nose.

'Wa-arghhhh!' I cried, leaping up, as there's one thing I don't like and that's creepy crawlies. And down here in Cornwall, there are plenty of them.

Jade was standing by the bed laughing. With the headphones on, I hadn't heard her come in and she'd been pushing a pencil up my nose.

'Phone,' she announced.

'Ever heard of knocking?' I asked.

'Did. You didn't answer. Probably too upset over the break up, huh?'

'Who is it?' I asked, ignoring her comment. That was another thing I didn't like about being down here. At my old school there were over a thousand pupils and you could go about your business without everyone knowing it. The school here is much smaller and the slightest bit of gossip and it spreads like the Asian flu. If it had got to Jade already then most of school would know that I'd been dumped by tomorrow.

'You'll see. A blast from the past,' she said, then smiled insincerely. 'Not Becca. *Obviously.*'

Jade can be a right cow sometimes. Most times actually. And she was really mean to Becca last year when they both went in for a Pop Princess competition. She's always had it in for her. I reckon she's jealous as Becca is popular and Jade likes to think that she's Queen Bee. She's already got her own little clique of Year Ten wannabees round her at school. She likes to swan about as if she knows what's cool because she went to school in London but like me, by now she's probably way out of touch. All of them want to be models and can only ever talk blond highlights, handbags and pointy shoes.

'Actually it was mutual between Bec and I. A joint decision,' I said as I went down to the hall and picked up the phone. (Gran hasn't got a portable yet.)

'Yeah, right,' Jade called after me. 'Sounds more to me like she finally got her eyesight back.'

'Hello?'

'Hi, Mac. It's me,' said the voice at the other end of the line.

'Me?'

'Yeah. Me. Don't you recognise my voice?'

'Er . . . Nope.'

'It's *Roz*. Roz Williams. Remember?'

'Oh *yeah*. Right. Roz. Hey, long time.'

It had been years since I'd seen Roz. We used to go to the same junior school up in London and later, Mum used to cater for her parents' posh dinner parties. She was a skinny little thing. Dead bossy and more Jade's friend than mine. I remember how she used to like to play teachers and pupils. Course she was always the teacher and she would line me and my mates up in her bedroom and whack us with her Barbie doll if we didn't do as she said. She was funny. Annoying, but funny. We've e-mailed a few times and I usually send her one of my cartoon cards for her birthday and Christmas as she seems to like getting them. Also, I suspect that she's behind a couple of the Valentine cards I've received in the last couple of years. I reckon she always had a bit of a crush on me, although no way is she my type.

'Yes. Years,' she said. 'How you doing down there?'

'Yeah, great. Love it,' I lied. 'So how are you?'

'Good. I'm good. Listen, reason I'm calling is that I have something to tell you that you might be *veeeery* interested in. You know Dad is features editor at *Kudos*?'

'Yeah.' Course I did. *Kudos* was huge. Everyone had heard of it.

'Well, in one of the autumn editions, they're going to be doing a supplement on teen talent. People to watch, that sort of thing . . .'

'Cool. I'll get a copy when it comes out.'

'No, listen, stupid. I thought of you.'

'*Me?* Why?'

'Just listen. They're going to do a spread on four up-and-coming new faces. All teenagers. A singer-songwriter, an actor, a writer and an artist. They'll probably be photographed but I suggested that, as the supplement is about teen talent, it might be cool if they got a teenage cartoonist to do caricatures of the people featured. Dad loved the idea and I showed him some of the cards you've sent me and suggested you. He said he'd have a look at your stuff. Course, there will be other people pitching for it as well but your cartoons are brill. I'm sure you'd get it.'

Yeah, right, I thought. As if her dad would give a gig like that to a boy just because his daughter fancied him. My first instinct was to say, no, I can't do it. They're bound to be looking for a professional, not some kid living in the back of beyond in Cornwall.

'But I've never even sent any of my cartoons off anywhere, to any kind of publication . . .'

'So now's the time to start.'

'And this is GCSE year, I have a ton of homework already and . . . I don't know, Roz. Look, I'll be honest. I'm not up in London any more and I can't just up and . . .'

'So what do you do down there all the time? Not a lot by what Jade told me before. What would you be doing next weekend that would be more important for your future career? Just homework?'

She had a point. What would I be doing? Trying to avoid Becca and the rest of the peninsula until the gossip about us had become old news. Another weekend wandering the ghost town and waiting for the summer when at least some tourists start to pass through.

'I guess, we don't do much. Jade's right. Not much happening down here at all. In fact, it's so quiet that we've had to resort to playing daft games like Truth, Dare, Kiss or Promise.'

'You're kidding? We used to play that in junior school.'

'Tell me about it. Cornwall's not exactly the happening place. It only comes to life in the summer. Although we did have a film crew down here in the Easter holidays.'

Roz wasn't listening. 'Truth, Dare, huh? OK. Can anyone play?'

'Yeah, although it's usually just me, Squidge and . . .'

'OK, then. Count me in. I've got something to add to your game. A double dare. I double dare that you go for the cartooning job and come up to London to stay here and take me out somewhere. We've got loads of room so it won't be a problem.'

I laughed. Same old bossy Roz. She hadn't changed a bit.

'We could take in a movie, hang out at Camden Lock . . .'

She was beginning to get to me as the tempting possibility of a weekend in London played through my mind. I could see my old mates. Revisit all my favourite hang-outs. See what's happening at the Tate. Maybe even talk to Dad about going back up there to live. Better to talk it over in person with him than sending the letter that I 'd only got started up at the café. But how would I get to London? Mum would never agree. No. It wasn't going to happen.

'Look, Roz, I'm seriously grateful that you thought of me but I don't th—'

'Too late. I've double dared you. And it was my idea. I'm going to look at right fool having talked Dad into it then my main contender won't come through. Remember when we used to play 'School' and I used to whack you with my Barbie if you'd been misbehaving?'

'Oh yeah,' I said, laughing. 'I've still got the scars.'

'Well, I've still got her. I've got her in my hand right now and her golden locks are swishing through the air as we speak, ready to whack you if you don't come. And I did double dare you. I remember the rules of the game. You can't go back on it or you'll have bad luck for a trillion years.'

I laughed again. 'Fair point,' I said. 'And although I don't want the shame of death by nylon tresses or a trillion years bad luck, I just can't . . .'

'No such word as "can't". No one ever tell you that? Come on, go for it. Don't be a wuss.'

'Look, I'll try, OK? That's all I can say. I'll try. But I'd like to stay with my dad if I come as I don't get to see him that often and . . .'

'Fair enough. But you'll still take me out somewhere?'

'I'll still take you out somewhere, that is *if* I come.'

'*When* you come, not if. I'll let Dad know that you'll be coming up to see him. He said next Saturday would be good. When the magazine gets started on something like this, they don't hang around. It will be such a brilliant experience for you. A taster of what it's going to be like when you're working full time.'

The idea was beginning to appeal more and more. 'I'll call you and let you know what's happening,' I said.

I felt fused with energy by the time I'd put the phone down. A weekend in London. And if I stayed with Dad, I could broach the idea of me coming to London for my A-levels. It wouldn't be so hard if I had to see Roz for an hour or so. And I'd meet with her dad, I owed her that. No way would he give me the cartooning gig. It just wouldn't happen, but a weekend away would be perfect.

Now all I needed to do was put the idea to Mum.

3   *Hubble Bubble*

MY OWN CARTOONING GIG in a major glossy! I could feel the adrenaline starting to flow as my imagination went into overdrive. It would be brilliant on my CV and would no doubt help me get a place at a top art college. And the acclaim that would go with it. Oh man. It would raise my babe appeal no end. I read in one of Jade's girlie mags, that after a GSOH (good sense of humour), the next thing that girls are attracted to is talent. What better proof of talent than my own work published? I could flash the supplement around or better still, leave it in places where people would come across it, like the school library. The news would soon spread round the area.

'Did you hear about Tom Macey? The boy that Becca dumped. He was way out of her league. Have you seen the cartoons he did in *Kudos*? Brilliant.'

'And he's only sixteen. Got a place at St Martin's, I believe. Only the best get in there.'

'I always thought he had something special. Wonder if he's single?'

Oh yes, Roz Williams. An hour or so with you will be well worth the effort.

I pulled my portfolio out from behind my desk and had a quick flick through. So what's in here? I asked myself as I laid my work out on the floor.

There was a whole bunch of superheroes from when I was in Year Seven and Eight. Superman, Batman, Spider-Man – I was really into them back then but I've moved on since. They aren't bad but they don't show much individual style (mainly because I copied them from comics). But I remembered what Mr Barnes, our art teacher, said about preparing our portfolio for college interviews. He said to put in a variety of work so that the interviewer can see that you are versatile.

Next was a load of stuff from when I went through my *Simpsons* phase and everyone I drew looked like Homer, Marge, Bart or Lisa.

A load of cards for Christmas and birthdays. Yeah, one or two of them are worth putting in. And I'd won a prize for one I'd done in Year Ten. It was of the bunch of snowmen, singing, 'There's no business like snow business'.

Couple of cartoon strips, the kind of thing you see in the tabloids. Yeah, I'll bung one of them in.

Pages and pages of hands and feet. There's a real art to getting cartoon hands and feet right and I was good at them. Maybe won't put them in though, I decided, as I reckoned Mr Williams was going to want more proof of skill than a drawing of the perfect cartoon foot.

Pages of special effects: cold, hot, melting, wet, shiny, smoke.

People of different nationalities: Scottish, Chinese, Italian, African, French, German.

Loads of individual drawings of people of different shapes and sizes.

Drawings of all the clichés: clowns, vampires, drunks, fools, evil, tarty, handsome rogue.

Cartoons showing movement.

Cartoons showing that I understood perspective. One-, two-, three-dimensional.

Cartoon cars, animals, landscapes.

Cartoons blocked out for animation.

Cartoons showing all the emotions: happy, sad, sleepy, angry, determined, shocked, concerned, sheepish, gloomy. There are techniques to showing what someone's feeling in a cartoon and they don't take long to learn. It's just a question of where you put the eyebrows sometimes. High on the forehead for surprised. Low and angled in towards the nose for angry. I'd put a few of them in, I decided, as they showed that I'd grasped the techniques.

I had a good collection of work. There was just one element that was missing. Caricatures. We'd only done a couple of classes on them so far and they are the most difficult of all to do.

'People can either do these or not,' said Mr Barnes. 'Lots of famous cartoonists shy away from them so don't be discouraged if it's not your bag.'

There were a few pages of my feeble attempts at caricaturing other pupils in my class, but nothing I could put into my portfolio with any confidence. Then I remembered, there was one. It was a drawing I'd done of Gran when she started going to line dancing. I'd drawn her dressed as a cowgirl complete with boots, stetson and a lasso. I was worried about showing it to her in case she was insulted, but she loved it and hung it in the downstairs loo. She's a right character, is my gran. She's in her sixties but she's not one of these stay-at-home oldies who are in every night by the telly with their cocoa and their knitting. No. She's out most nights. Line dancing on Monday. Bridge on Tuesday. She works in the library Wednesday. Does a mobile library on Thursday. Pilates on Friday, runs a craft stall on Saturday and goes rambling with a group on

Sundays. I couldn't keep up with her. Though sometimes I wonder if the fact that she's out so much is due to the fact that Mum, Jade and I have taken over her house.

I was so absorbed in sorting my work into piles that I didn't hear Mum come in.

'What's all this?' she asked.

'Oh. Work. Getting my portfolio together.'

'What for? I would have thought you had ages before you needed to get this ready.'

No time like the present, I thought as I took a deep breath and told her about my conversation with Roz.

She sat on the end of the bed. 'Sounds good. So will they send you some photos of these people so that you can work from them?'

'I haven't got the job yet, Mum. I have to go and pitch. Have to go to London. But it will be brilliant on my CV for applying to college.'

'No doubt. Sounds professional. Serious. And Mr Williams has a great reputation. Well, I suppose you could go at half-term as you were planning to go and see your father then, anyway.'

'That will be too late. I have to go this weekend.'

'This weekend? No. You've only just gone back to school. Absolutely not.'

'But I have to . . .'

'What's going on?' asked Gran, appearing in the hallway. She must be back from line dancing, I thought, as she spotted my work. 'Can I come in and look?'

Before waiting for an answer, she was in and, with a creak, was kneeling down to examine my work.

'Mac wants to go to London this weekend,' said Mum and proceeded to fill Gran in on the story, as if I wasn't there.

And then Jade walked in to join them. 'What's all this mess?' she said as she plonked herself next to Mum on my bed and looked over my work. I winced – normally, I don't like my family looking at my work and giving their opinions, and now here were three of them sifting through it like it was public property, while Gran filled Jade in.

'If he's going I'm going,' she said. 'Roz was more my friend than his.'

'He's not going,' said Mum.

'I think you should let him go,' said Gran. 'Not often opportunities like this present themselves.'

'There's no way he can go. He's just back at school.'

'But it's the weekend,' said Gran. 'Be up and back in no time.'

'I'd love a weekend up in London,' said Jade. 'We could both stay at Dad's or with Roz.'

'He has homework. This is GCSE year. And he wasted enough time on the film set at Easter,' said Mum.

'He could do it on the train,' said Gran. 'Three hours there, three hours back. He could get a ton done.'

'And you're not going either, Jade. No need to pout like that. I've said no to both of you and that's my final word.'

Three generations of mad women and I have to live with them, I thought, as I watched them squabbling between themselves. What did I ever do to deserve this? Three generations of knickers in the laundry room, cosmetics in the bathroom, girlie CDs on the sound system. A weekend with my dad and my mates was just what I needed. Some solid male company.

'No, Mac,' said Mum as the three of them finally remembered that I was there and turned to me. 'That's my final word.'

'You go, Mac,' said Gran. 'Show them what you've got.'

'And I'm coming with you,' said Jade.

'And where would you get the train fare? I'm not made of money,' said Mum.

'It's your birthday soon. I'll give it to you,' said Gran. 'Early present.'

'Shall I check out train times?' asked Jade.

A drawing was beginning to form in my head. I wanted them out of the room so that I could start it. My gran, my mum and my sister as the three mad witches in *Macbeth*. Hubble bubble, toil and trouble. Three mad blondes. One old, one young, one in the middle. The three of them cackling and stirring a big pot over a fire. And sitting in that pot was me . . .

When I'd finally got rid of them, I tried Dad's number but it was on answerphone. I tried his mobile but it was on voicemail. I didn't leave a message as I knew he'd agree to let me stay. He was the easy part of the deal. Being an artist himself, he was bound to see the opportunity and he'd always been supportive of my work.

I began to draw the three witches. Just as I'd sketched Mum, Gran popped her head round the door and gave me the thumbs up.

'Sorted,' she said and handed me fifty pounds.

'Wow. Thanks. But how?'

Gran tapped her nose. 'I have my ways.'

I laughed. 'Thanks, Gran.'

'You just get up there and show them what you can do. If it's anything like my "lasso lady in the loo", you're in business.'

Brilliant, I thought as she closed the door. London, here I come.

4   Change of Plan

'TOM MACEY. ARE YOU AWAKE?'

It sounded as if someone was breaking my door down so I pulled my duvet over my head and snuggled down deeper into bed.

'I'm up. I'm *up*. And I'm not deaf.'

I heard Mum's sarcastic snort and footsteps retreating. I poked my head out of the covers and glanced at the clock. Oops. Overslept. I hauled myself out of bed and stepped carefully over the mass of drawings and collection of used mugs that were still all over the floor from last night. Over on my desk was the drawing of the three witches of Anderton. Jade would kill me if anyone from school saw it. Heh, heh, I thought as I let myself out of my room and padded along the wooden floor to the bathroom. I could get to like this caricature business. It was a great way to let off steam.

Mum was busy feeding a couple of B&B guests in the dining room when I got down, so I took my mobile, went out the french windows in the living room and into the back garden where I could phone Dad in private. He picked up immediately.

'Dad. It's me.'

'Mac. How are you?'

'Fine. You?'

'Fine. It's rather early to be calling. Where are you?'

'Sitting under the rose pergola at Gran's.'

'Something the matter?'

'No. Well, yes. I need to talk to you about something.'

'Oh . . . Can it wait? I'm just about to take Tamara to school.'

I couldn't help but feel a stab of envy. He never used to take Jade or me to school when we were up there and we're his real kids.

'Won't take a moment,' I said and quickly filled him in on the cartooning job.

'Sounds good. You go for it. Look . . .'

'I will. I've started drawings already. But can I stay at yours? Saturday? I know Tamara's in the spare room but I can crash in your office or on the sofa.'

There was an awkward silence at the other end of the phone. 'Oh, Mac. Any other weekend, but Tamara's got a sleepover planned for this Saturday. Eight mates, God help us. There will be bodies everywhere. Isn't there anywhere else you could stay? Max or Andy? One of your old pals?'

Yeah right, I thought. Like I'm going to tell them that my own father won't put me up. It would be one thing asking my mates to meet up in the day, another having to admit that I'd been usurped by an eight-year-old.

'Not really.'

'Listen, son, I really do have to get going. You know what these school runs are like. Sonia will kill me if I'm late.'

'OK. Er . . . Dad. Just one more thing. I . . . I . . . You know this is GCSE year. I wanted to put something to you. I'll be quick. I want to apply to colleges in London. What about I stay with you for my A-level years? No need to decide this morning. Just think about it?'

Another awkward silence. 'A-levels?' he said after a few moments. 'Doesn't time fly? But . . . bit short of space up here, you know that. Look. I don't know. I'll think about it. We'll talk about it in the half-term when you come up. Things might be different by then. Have you talked to your mother about it?'

'No.'

'Right . . . OK. Got to fly. We'll talk about it. I'll call you.'

Yeah sure, I thought as I put the phone down. Message received loud and clear. I'm not wanted there. Talk about let down. I felt totally deflated. Ah well, I told myself as I shuffled back into the house to grab my school bag, maybe I'll just buy a new pair of jeans with the fifty quid Gran gave me. I need a new pair.

'You've got to go for it, man,' said Squidge after I'd filled him in at break at school. 'You'd be mental not to.'

'Nah. Roz would have me for breakfast if I stayed there. You don't know her. One of those girls who will always get their way. She'll probably be prime minister by the time she's thirty.'

'And your dad said no to you being up there for your A-levels?'

'Dad never says no exactly. He just gives vague answers until you give up trying. Mum, on the other hand, gives you a ten-point plan of action. No wonder they split up. I think Dad's indecisiveness was one of the reasons Mum got so fed up him. She found it took less time to do things herself while he dilly-dallied about making up his mind. Trouble was, in the end, she was doing everything. Accounts, main breadwinner, running the house. My theory is that that is why he had the affair. He felt emasculated.'

'Ooh, get you and your big words,' said Squidge.

'No. Seriously. I read about it in one of Gran's *Good Housekeeping* mags. An article about how when women become the main earners, it can leave their men feeling like failures and often leads to them going astray to assert their masculinity.'

Squidge cracked up. 'Since when have you been reading *Good Housekeeping?*'

I punched his arm. 'Well, there's bugger all else to do down here in the winter.'

'Oh, get a life, saddo,' said Squidge. 'Someone offers you a chance like this and you're acting like a limp lettuce. Oh, my dad doesn't want me, oh, my mum's an ogre.'

'Talking of which,' I said as I pulled my latest drawing out of my bag, 'I have something to show you. What do you think?'

He took the paper and laughed out loud. 'Brilliant. Hey, Mac, this is seriously good. Has Jade seen it?'

'No way. She'd kill me.'

Squidge scrutinised the drawing carefully. 'No, mate. I mean it. This is good. You have to go to London. So this girl double dared you, did she?'

I rolled my eyes. 'Yeah.'

'And you know the rules . . .'

'A trillion years bad luck if I don't do it.'

'I was going to say a million but I guess as it's a double

dare, she's probably right, a trillion. Listen. Do a few more drawings like this and I reckon you'll be in with a good chance. I know caricature is hard but it looks like you have the knack. Draw everyone we know. And do a few of famous people so the editor bloke can see how good you are.'

It was great having Squidge to talk to about stuff like this. I respect his opinion and he understands. He wants to do photography or film directing when he leaves school and although they are different mediums to cartooning, he knows about capturing images in different ways. We have great plans about going to the same college and getting a babe magnet flat with a pinball and juke box and loads of people passing through (mainly girls). I could feel my enthusiasm beginning to return.

'Yeah, good idea. Do a few celebs. If I pick a few with strong features, they shouldn't be hard to do.'

'Yeah, like Prince Charles with his sticky-out ears.'

'Or Brad Pitt with his strong jaw.'

Squidge knew the rules as I did. With caricature, you took someone's features and exaggerated the hell out of them. The ones that worked best were of people with easily identifiable features like Jack Nicholson with his mad eyebrows, Michael Jackson with his high hair line and tiny nose or Mick Jagger with his wide rubbery lips. The hard ones to do were of people with even features or bland faces as there was nothing to take to extremes.

Suddenly, I smacked my forehead. 'Carumba. I've just had the most *brilliant* idea. Why didn't I think of it before? Roz said that there was loads of room at her parents' house. You could come too. Be my chaperone in case Roz gets any funny ideas. You up for it? You must have some money left from working on the film set. What do you say? I could show you London.'

Squidge didn't hesitate. 'Yeah. Sure. I'd have to ask Mum and Dad but, hey, yeah, I'd love it. Just what we need after a first week back at school.'

'Cool. So staying at Dad's is out? Who needs him? We revert to plan B. You call your folks. And I'll call Roz.'

We quickly got on to our mobiles and five minutes later, Squidge was smiling.

'Result?' I asked.

'Result. Took a bit of persuasion but everyone has their price.'

'Which is?'

'I promised to babysit Amy next week. You have any luck?'

'Left a message on her voicemail. Shouldn't be a problem though. She said there was loads of room. And she'll love you.'

Excellent, I thought as the bell rang and we went back

into class. Having Squidge for company would make the journey all the more enjoyable, and he'd be a safety buffer between Roz and me.

I spent the rest of the day sketching teachers in my notepad when they weren't looking. By the time we were let out in the afternoon, I had one of Mr Barnes looking like an overstuffed and smiley little mouse, one of Mr Daley sitting on the branch of a tree looking like an angry eagle and one of Mrs Ross looking like a frog with big bulging eyes behind her glasses.

My interview material was coming together nicely.

'So what's all this about a trip to London?' asked Becca, appearing out of nowhere as I stood at the bus stop after school.

'Oh, hey, Becca,' I said, suddenly realising that I hadn't thought about her all day. How was I supposed to behave? 'Yeah. Squidge and me.'

'And who's this Roz?'

The Asian flu has been spreading as usual, I thought, as I tried to decide what to tell her. No doubt, Squidge had told Lia, Lia told Cat, Cat told Becca. Same old story. Just at that moment, my mobile rang. It was Roz. She sounded flustered.

'Mac. I'm so sorry. When I told Mum you might be

coming last night she went into a panic. Apparently, she's invited a pile of people this weekend. Hadn't got round to telling Dad. I'm so sorry. I'd love to meet Squidge. I could book him into a hotel if you like?'

That cracked me up. 'Doubt if he'd have that kind of money, Roz.'

'But you can still stay if you don't mind sleeping on the sofa-bed in the office downstairs.'

'Let me talk to Squidge.'

'Call me tonight.'

'OK.

'About eight.'

'OK.'

I clicked my phone shut to see that Becca had been listening in.

'So was that her?'

I nodded.

'Well, you don't waste any time, do you?' she said, pouting.

Oh God, I thought. She's upset. Maybe she regrets having dumped me.

She flicked her hair and gave me a flirtatious look. Oh God, I thought in a sudden panic. She wants me back.

'Roz is an old mate. I'm maybe going to be staying with her.'

'And how old is she?'

'Your age.'

Becca looked miffed so I put my arm around her. 'She's not a patch on you,' I said, to try and make her feel better. 'You don't need to think I'll be getting off with her.'

Becca wriggled away from my arm. 'Oh, but I think you should,' she said. 'I've been feeling sooo responsible since yesterday. Another girl will help you get over me so I just wanted to say, you carry on. Don't worry about me at all.'

Jesus almighty. Talk about ego. If there was an Olympic prize for it, Becca would win the gold.

'Thanks I will,' I said. If she was going to be like that about it, then I wasn't going to tell her that the truth was that Roz was no way fanciable.

Luckily, we were saved by the bus and as it came round the corner, Squidge came flying out of the school gates and we both exited fast.

'Girls,' I said as we sat at the back. 'I'll never get what goes on in their strange heads.'

'Don't even try,' said Squidge. 'And talking of which, Lia. She wants to come to London with us. So . . . slight change of plan. She's going to ask her sister, Star, if I can crash at her place in Notting Hill Gate with her. She's asking her parents tonight.'

'Do you ever feel that your life is taken over by women?' I asked.

Squidge rolled his eyes. 'Tell me about it.'

'Maybe I could stay at Star's with you?'

'I can ask, but she's only got a one bedroom place. We'll be sleeping under the sink as it is.'

Bugger, I thought. Looks like Roz is going to get her way.

London

5

'YAHEY, I'M HOME,' I said as the familiar sights of London began to flash past the train window. Rows and rows of houses. Endless high-rise blocks of flats, busy streets clogged with the usual Friday night traffic. Soon we were arriving into Paddington Station. It felt great to be back as we hauled our luggage down from the overhead rack and joined the other travellers in the corridor waiting to get off the train.

'So what does Roz look like?' asked Lia, as we made our way down the platform.

'Haven't seen her for years,' I said. 'Skinny. Pale. Dark.'

Squidge nudged me. 'So all set for a weekend of passion?'

'No *way*,' I said. 'She'd never be my type. Not in a million years.'

'Are her mum or dad coming to meet you as well?' asked Squidge.

'Don't think so. She said she'd come and we'd get a cab back. Her family are loaded. And anyway, they've got guests so are probably busy with them. At least Roz won't be able to pounce on me if there are people around.'

As we walked through the station, past the ticket guards and into the busy crowd of commuters all in a rush to get home, I scanned faces for anyone resembling the Roz I used to know, but couldn't see anyone. Suddenly, a girl flew out of nowhere and before I knew it, I was being smothered in a perfumed embrace.

'Wah –'

'Mac,' said the girl. 'You look great.'

'And you . . .' I could hardly believe my eyes. 'Roz . . . you look . . . well . . . different.'

Roz did a twirl. She was wearing a pleated denim mini skirt, a tight pink T-shirt with 'Princess' emblazoned across it in silver and her hair was a glossy chestnut, halfway down her back. She was no longer the skinny kid with legs like sticks. Her legs were great. And she'd filled out. In all the right places.

'Are you going to introduce me to your friends?' she asked as she looked at Lia and Squidge.

'Oh yeah. Lia, Squidge, this is Roz.'

Just as they were saying hi, Lia spotted her sister and rushed across to give her a hug. Even dressed in jeans and a T-shirt, Star stood out in the crowd. She's a top model on all the covers of the glossies. She looks just like Lia, face like an angel, same white-blond hair, silver blue eyes, only her hair is cut short whereas Lia's is long.

Roz's mouth dropped open. 'Ohmigod. That's Star Axford. *Star* Axford.' She charged across to join Lia. 'Hi. I'm Roz. A friend of Mac's.'

Star looked a bit startled. 'Oh hi. And oh . . . there's Squidge. Hi, Squidge. So you guys ready? I'm on a meter.'

'Yeah,' said Squidge as he picked up Lia's bag and gave me a wink. 'Catch you later.'

'Yes,' said Roz butting in. 'Maybe we could all meet up? Have you got my number?'

'Er, Mac's got it,' said Squidge as he began to follow Lia and Star across the station. 'Be in touch Mac.'

'Yes, we will,' said Roz as they waved goodbye and disappeared into the crowd.

'I can't *believe* that you know *Star* Axford,' said Roz as she gazed after them. 'She's like mega. I thought you said nothing happened down in Cornwall.'

'She's Lia's sister.'

'So you know the whole family? Ohmigod. Ohmigod. We *have* to meet up with them. No one at school will believe it.'

Lia's family is notorious. As well as having a sister who's a top model, her dad is the famous rock star Zac Axford. Lia's parents moved down to Cornwall a few months after me, leaving Lia and her older brother, Ollie, at school in London. Lia hated being so far away from her mum and dad and asked if she could go to a local school but Ollie stayed where he was. I thought she was mad leaving London but she says she's loads happier. The Axfords caused quite a stir when they first arrived and were the talk of all the villages. But we soon got used to having a celeb family down there with us, especially as, apart from the occasional glam party, they live a quiet life and aren't posey or anything naff like that.

'So come on,' said Roz pulling me towards the cab rank. 'Let's get going and you can tell me all about them.'

On the way back in the taxi, I realised that Roz might have changed looks-wise but she was still the same old Roz. Bossy as ever. She had an itinerary worked out for the whole weekend and I soon saw my own plans to meet up with Max and Andy going out the window.

'And we have to meet up with Star again,' said Roz as the taxi drove west and out towards Richmond where the Williamses now lived. 'Maybe we could all go out together somewhere.'

'Sure, sure,' I said. Anything to keep the peace. I was so happy to be back on my old turf, I would have agreed to anything.

'How about tomorrow? You're seeing Dad at his office at twelve so how about we meet for breakfast. Phone them now, see what they're doing.'

'What, now? They won't be back at Star's yet.'

'Yes, but they might be making their own plans so we need to get in there fast.'

I got out my mobile. I didn't feel I could refuse seeing as I owed Roz for putting me up and getting me in to see her dad. And maybe going out for breakfast would count as me taking Roz out on a date of sorts. Safety in numbers. I could see I was going to need them.

Roz's place was fabulous. A tall terraced Georgian house on Richmond Hill with a stunning view of the River Thames winding away into the distance at the back. As befitting a features editor on a major lifestyle magazine, everywhere was done out with exquisite taste, each room themed to a different culture: an elegant red and cream living room with golden Thai artefacts; an ochre Moroccan den with low kilm-covered sofas and rugs on the walls and floor. Enormous expensive looking art books arranged on the coffee tables. White airy bathrooms as big as bedrooms.

I'm going to enjoy staying here, I thought. It was like walking into a five star hotel. The flower arrangements alone looked like they cost more than I get in pocket money in a year.

'You're not the only one with rock star neighbours. Mick Jagger has a place just up the road,' said Roz after she'd given me the tour and led me into a state-of-the-art kitchen. It was different to the rest of the house. Austere with minimalist décor and the total opposite of our comfy country kitchen back in Cornwall with its Aga, pine dining table and dresser displaying Gran's collection of Clarice Cliff pottery.

'This is cool,' I said as I sat on a chrome stool at the black granite breakfast bar and took in the subtle lighting, stainless steel splash backs and immaculate surfaces. 'Although it looks more like a hospital operating theatre than a kitchen.'

'Well, you remember what Mummy's like. Likes to eat. Hates to cook. I don't think she ever recovered when your mum left London. She never found a replacement she was happy with to do her dinner parties.'

'Where is everyone? I thought your mum was having guests.'

'Taken them out for dinner. I told you Mummy doesn't cook. And you must be starving. I think there's some

snacky stuff in here or Mummy said we could get takeaway.'
She opened an enormous American style fridge, had a root
around, then quickly closed it. 'No. Takeaway. I fancy
sushi.'

I hate sushi but didn't want to appear to be rude.
'Whatever,' I said. 'You choose.'

While we were waiting for our food to arrive, I offered to
show Roz some of my drawings. Over the week, I'd
managed to get a decent collection together. Most of my
teachers, the witches at home, the one of Gran as a cowgirl,
Squidge, Lia, Becca and Cat and a few of famous people,
Prince Charles, George W. Bush, Princess Anne, Jacko,
Mick Jagger.

She came and sat very close to me on the sofa and seemed
well impressed.

'Who are these two?' she asked, pointing at the drawings
of Becca and Cat. I'd redrawn the one I'd started up at the
View café on the Monday after school but exaggerated the
girls' features a bit more.

'Oh, my mates. We all hang out.'

'No serious girlfriend, then?' she asked as she leaned over
me to study the drawings and let her hair brush over my
arm. She smelled great.

'Um . . .' I didn't want to say yes or no in case she got
ideas about us having a relationship. She moved a fraction

closer on the sofa. This was the moment I'd been dreading. I just didn't think she'd do it so soon . . . but now it was happening, I found I didn't mind that much. OK, she was bossy, but she had great hair and . . . those legs . . .

She'd let a curtain of hair fall over her face and looked up at me flirtatiously from behind it.

If you can't beat them, join them, I thought. OK, so she's not exactly my type. I tend to like girls with soft features whereas Roz's face is angular like her dad's, with a sharp nose and small mouth. But no doubt, the whole package was attractive. Why not? I asked myself. I'm young, I'm single. Part of the reason I wanted to break up with Becca was because I wanted more experience with girls. And Roz clearly wants me. Has done since she was nine. As she was rambling on about something, she lightly put her hand on my thigh. Definitely a come on, I thought so I put my arm around her.

She stiffened and pushed me away. 'Wo*ah*,' she said. 'Easy.'

'Wha . . .? I . . . I thought you wanted to . . .'

She moved a fraction away on the sofa. 'Maybe I do. Maybe I don't. *I'll* say when.'

I felt my stomach churn. I couldn't be doing with girls who played games. And she was making it very clear that in this game, she made the rules. I'd got it wrong again. I really thought she was moving in on me. Giving me the come on. What was I supposed to think?

The doorbell went, announcing that our food had arrived so Roz jumped up to get it. I wondered what Squidge was doing and wished I was with him. Probably having a fab, relaxed time somewhere with Star and Lia and here was I, holed up with another control freak with a supper of raw fish to look forward to.

Woopeedoop.

6

Sergeant Major

'TOM MACEY, ARE YOU UP?'

'I'm up, I'm *up*,' I said as I pulled the duvet over my head and snuggled down deeper into the bed.

The voice sounded familiar but something wasn't right.

I sat up and opened my eyes. Where was I? In a small office-type room with floor to ceiling bookshelves and a desk and a computer. Not at home. I was at Roz's. Of course. Jesus, I thought, she has exactly the same tone of command in her voice as Mum. I pushed the duvet off, got out of bed and began to scramble into my jeans. Roz burst in, carrying a mug of tea.

'Wo*ah*, hold on . . .' I said as I hopped around on one leg. 'Not dressed.'

Roz looked me up and down. 'I can see that. Nice shorts.' She grinned and put the tea on the desk. 'Dad's gone already but he said to be at the office in Soho twelve o'clock sharp. I'll take you. We're meeting Star and your mates at ten near Portobello Road for breakfast so we'll get the District line tube. Takes us straight there and it will be quicker than taking a cab at this time of day. So we'd better get going soon. Fifteen minutes. That'll give you time to use the bathroom.'

I zipped my jeans, gave her a salute and stood to attention. 'Yes, sergeant major, sir. Reporting for duty, sir.'

She gave me a look as if to say I was mad then with a toss of her hair, flounced out.

Squidge, Lia and Star were already waiting for us outside the tube station at Notting Hill Gate so we made our way up to the market together. Portobello Road on a Saturday was one of my favourite haunts. Busy market stalls selling everything from joss sticks, Indian paraphernalia, fruit and veg, antiques, clothes, jewellery, picture frames . . . you name it. As always it was swarming with people browsing, buying, enjoying the atmosphere and the spring sunshine.

'Survived the night, I see,' said Squidge as Roz and the girls walked ahead where I could hear Roz grilling Star about her job as a model.

'Just about. Sometimes I feel that my destiny in life is to be taken over by dominant women. Are they all like that?'

'Different degrees. They call the shots most of the time, especially if they're lookers.'

'Lia like that?'

Squidge shook his head. 'Nah. She's not bossy. But then I am more than willing to be her slave and do whatever she wants.'

I sighed. 'I just want to have a bit of fun. You know, no ties, no commitment. No *games*. When it starts getting heavy, I can't deal with their heads.'

'Yeah, you say that, but just you wait. One day you'll fall in love and then you won't mind.'

'Maybe when I'm about thirty. But until then I just wish I could find someone who felt the same way and doesn't come over all complicated or emotional. So far, all girls have done is confuse me. Do my head in.'

'You didn't seem to mind being with Becca at first and if any girl can be confusing, it's her.'

'Yeah, but it wasn't the big L with her. I *liked* her a lot. A *lot*. Still do. But it wasn't love. It was never like you and Lia. I know that's the real thing. So far, I've never felt anything remotely like that. Maybe I never will. In fact, tell you what I'd like when we get back. A night out, just you and me. No girls.'

'What going on the pull or something?'

'Down there? I don't think so. Nowhere to go. Let's do

something just us lads. Go camping or something. No women telling us what to do and when to do it.'

Squidge laughed. 'Last night was that bad, was it? Yeah, sure. Be good. Camping. We could go up to Rame Head. Next weekend's a Bank holiday, maybe we could go then.'

'For now, though, I think we'd better catch the girls up. I think Roz is hoping to manoeuvre a visit to Star's flat so that she can tell all her mates at school she went there.'

We hurried to catch the girls up and I made an effort to talk to Star, so that she wasn't totally monopolised by a starstruck Roz. Not that I wasn't starstruck myself. I've fancied Star from day one. She's sooo beautiful, graceful and elegant and even though I'd met her a few times already, I still found myself going all googly-eyed when she spoke to me. A fact that Roz soon picked up on. Just as I was having a nice chat with Star and telling her about my drawings, Roz butted in and pulled me away to look in a shop window.

'Maa*aac*,' she said in a whiny voice.

'What?'

'You're flirting with Star,' she pouted.

'I am not.'

'Oh yes you are. You fancy her, don't you?'

'Who wouldn't?'

'Well, how do you think that makes me feel?'

'You . . .? I . . . what do you mean?'

'It makes me look like a fool. Like you're with me and yet you're flirting with someone else.'

I was gobsmacked. Last night she hadn't even let me put my arm around her, never mind snog her. And now she was carrying on as if we were in some kind of serious relationship.

'I was just being friendly. She's Lia's sister, for heaven's sake, and she's way older than me.'

'Well, cool it, will you?'

I wanted to kill her or walk off there and then. But I'd come this far and we had the meeting with her dad set up. A plan started to hatch in my head as a reaction to her being so stroppy. Last night, when she asked if I had a serious girlfriend down in Cornwall, I'd evaded the question. I'd tell her that I did. Becca. And I'd ask Becca to support me. If Roz thought I was attached maybe she'd back off. Becca had said she'd do anything to help and while she was feeling responsible for my state of mind, I reckoned I could get her to agree.

Roz went back over to Lia and Star and I acted out strangling her behind her back.

'What's going on?' asked Squidge.

'She's only just given me the third degree for flirting with Star. Can you believe it? She's not even my girlfriend.'

Squidge laughed. 'Give her time. You said that she was a girl who gets what she wants. I can see what you mean now.'

I sighed and followed the girls into a café. Roz's choice, of course.

'You'll just love this place,' she said as she ushered Star in. 'I come here all the time with my mates.'

Personally, I would have asked Star the best place to go as she lives round here and if anyone knew the cool hangouts, I reckoned it would have been her. But like the rest of us, she wasn't asked.

After breakfast (which was good – chorizo sausage on ciabatta and a great cappuccino) Roz got up to go to the Ladies.

'Got you well under her thumb,' teased Star when Roz was out of earshot. 'Girls like that can take you over.'

'I can't reply until my mummy comes back from the Ladies,' I said.

Star and Lia laughed then Star leaned over and patted my hand.

'Next time, you can stay with us,' she said. 'We'll look after you.'

After a cruise round the market, Roz marched me back off towards the Tube to go to Soho.

She was a bit weird on the way there, linking her arm in mine and touching my arm or hand at every opportunity and I had a good idea that it wasn't just because the Tube was crowded that she kept pressing herself against me. I wasn't falling for it. I'd had enough of mixed messages. Even though she'd said that she'd let me know when I could come on to her, I didn't really want to. She was too much like hard work and as soon as the weekend was over, I wanted our relationship to go back to how it was before. Birthday and Christmas cards. And nothing in between.

Once she'd delivered me to her dad's office, she mercifully took off to do some shopping saying that she'd see me back in Richmond later in the afternoon.

At last I can breathe, I thought as she left me sitting in reception on the third floor. A few moments to prepare myself. A sudden attack of nerves hit me as I watched through the glass doors on the right. Even though it was a Saturday, the office was a hive of activity with people at computers, examining layouts, on the phone. They looked so assured and professional and suddenly, I felt out of my depth. Mr Williams will probably laugh me out of the office when he sees my work; I must be mad thinking I stand a chance, I thought as Roz's dad came out of an office to the left and indicated I should follow him back in.

'Tom,' he said as he closed the door behind us and shook

my hand. 'Sorry to have missed you last night and this morning. Busy time for the magazine. I trust that you were comfortable on the sofa bed.'

'Yes, thanks. Very comfortable.'

'And Roz looked after you?' he said looking at me closely.

I felt myself starting to blush and cursed myself. Nothing had gone on between us. Why was I acting like I'd just seduced his daughter?

'Er . . . yes, thank you.'

'And how's your mother?'

'Good. Fine.'

'Still cooking?'

'Yes.'

Mr Williams sat behind his desk and glanced at his watch. 'So. Roz tells me that you're a brilliant cartoonist.'

'Well . . . er . . .'

'So let's have a look. You've brought me some work, haven't you?'

I put my portfolio on his desk, opened it and took out the drawings I'd brought. He put on a pair of glasses, picked up the drawings and swung away slightly on his swivel chair to examine them.

I sat down and watched him. His face gave nothing away as he sifted through the pile. When he'd reached the last one, he tidied the pile, placed them back on the desk and looked at me. Still his face was expressionless.

Then he cracked a grin. 'Actually . . . not bad. Not bad at all. When Roz talked me into this, I agreed to keep her happy but I'm glad she did. Yes. Glad she did. Of course, there will be a number of other cartoonists pitching and the final decision isn't only down to me. I have to consult with my arts editor but . . . I'll put them forward. I trust you can leave them with me for a week or so. You've got copies, haven't you?'

'Er . . . no . . . I . . .'

Mr Williams shook his head. 'Lesson number one. Always take copies. I shall take care of your drawings but in the future, always have back-ups if you're submitting work anywhere. Anything can happen in an office like this. Coffee spilled, papers dumped by mistake, mixed up with others. I could give you a catalogue of disasters we've had with people's work.'

I nodded. 'Right. Will do.'

'Would you like to take a look at some of the other submissions I've had in? See what you're up against?'

I nodded again and he got up and went over to a desk at the side of his office.

'Come here,' he said and pulled out a couple of portfolios.

The first one was immaculate, with each piece of work

presented on laminated paper. Good drawings and, like me, the artist had submitted plenty of caricatures of famous people.

The second wasn't so neat but again, the drawing was good: showed an individual style. I could see that I had competition.

'We've got a bit of time on this,' said Mr Williams as he went back to his desk and glanced at my work again, 'and so far, I've been very impressed with the standard of work. And we've got a couple more submissions to come in. You'll be our youngest contender as the other lads are in sixth-form and one in his first year at art college but I'll put yours in there with them. Yes. Not bad at all.'

I wondered if he was being polite and going along with it to not hurt my feelings (or Roz's). I could understand him agreeing to meet me to please Roz but I knew he wouldn't commission anyone he felt wasn't up to the job just to keep her happy.

'Thank you. I really appreciate this,' I said, hoping that I didn't sound too much like a snivelling little sucker-upper.

'OK. So, these are the teens who we'll be featuring and you might be caricaturing,' he said, pulling a file out of a drawer in his desk. He took four photos from the file and passed them over to me.

'That's Otis, the artist,' he said as I looked at the top one.

'Eighteen years old and the next Damien Hirst, I'm told.' The photo was a moody black and white shot of a wiry looking boy with shoulder length curly hair, dressed in a leather jacket and jeans. He'd be great to draw, I thought. He had distinguishing features: dark bushy eyebrows, hooded sleepy eyes, a full Mick Jagger mouth and long Roman nose.

'Next is Alistair, our actor. Also eighteen, I believe.' His was a typical studio shot, in colour, this time. It showed a handsome boy with an even open face and short blond hair. He'd be hard to caricature, I thought. No outstanding features.

'And those are the girls, Emily Wells and Amanda Miller,' he continued as I got to the last two photos. 'Amanda on top, she's the singer-songwriter. Very good. Nice girl. Great voice, great future, I think. She's seventeen at present.'

I studied the photo trying to imagine how I'd draw her. She was a big black girl with a mass of wild curly hair, full mouth and big wide eyes. She had perfect features to exaggerate.

And then I looked at the last photograph: very pretty with a short, dark bob framing a delicate face. She had the look of a China doll. She looked nervous, like she didn't really want her picture to be taken.

'And that's Emily, the youngest at sixteen. Just had her

first children's book published to great acclaim.'

'Right. Thanks,' I said as I began to hand the pictures back to him.

'Those are yours to keep,' said Mr Williams. 'Take them away. Do a few preliminary sketches to show how you'd depict them and let us have them back as soon as you've got something. In the next couple of weeks or so, if possible. When we've got the work in from all of you, then we'll decide. So, you up for it?'

I nodded. 'Yes. Definitely.'

'Any questions?'

'Will I get to meet them? Get more of an idea of their characters. It would help . . .'

Mr Williams nodded. 'Good question. We have a meeting set up for all of the cartoonists to meet them next Friday night.'

He must have seen my face fall. There was no way I could come back up again for the meeting.

'Don't worry, Tom. The others all live in London and I know you can't make it. That's why I asked Roz to get you in today. You're in luck, because they're in for some studio shots. Come with me . . .'

The rest of the afternoon was a complete blast. Emily had already been in for her shots but I got to spend time with the other three 'new faces'. They were in a photography studio on the first floor and it seemed that no expense had been spared in looking after them. Plates of sandwiches, cookies that melted in your mouth, freshly baked blueberry muffins, fruit and whatever we wanted to drink on tap. While one of them was being lit and shot, the other two hung around and chatted. It was such a shame Squidge wasn't with me as he would have loved the buzz of being in a professional studio watching how it was done.

Amanda was brilliant, a natural exhibitionist and posed for the camera with ease. I liked her; she was larger than life in every sense and she played me one of her CDs whilst Alistair was being photographed. As Mr Williams had said, she had a great voice, strong and soulful with an incredible range. I could understand why she had been chosen. Her songs blew me away.

I liked Otis too. He was quieter than Amanda, unassuming, but he had something about him. Cool. Squidge would have liked him. He had brought some shots of his work along for the art editor. His work was a combination of painting and sculpture, all abstract. It was interesting.

Alistair, on the other hand, seemed like an arrogant prat. Tall, athletic and full of himself. He was clear about what he wanted, how he wanted to be shot and kept giving the lighting man directions. And when he heard that I might be one of the cartoonists, he gave me a long lecture on how I ought to depict him.

'Just do your own thing,' said Otis when Alistair went off to talk to the lighting man. 'Don't let him tell you what to do.'

I nodded. I wanted to get the job more than ever having been there and met the talent. There was an air of excitement around these guys and I wanted to be part of it.

By about four o'clock, things were wrapping up and people were getting ready to go. It was then that the studio door opened and a girl walked in.

I knew straight away that it was Emily. I recognised her from her picture but she looked way more fragile than in the photograph, like a waif in an ankle length flowery dress with a white flower pinned on her shoulder.

She glanced over at me. Our eyes met.

It was love at first sight.

7

Emily

'I'M HEADING FOR THE TUBE,' said Emily. 'We could walk together.'

Alistair, Amanda and Otis had gone off to see a movie in Leicester Square after everything had been wrapped up in the studio. They asked if I wanted to go along but I said no, as I knew that Roz was expecting me back. She'd already texted four times during the afternoon. Plus I didn't want to leave without speaking to Emily. She'd only come back to the office as she'd realised that she had left her mobile phone behind. Fate, I thought. Destiny. She might think she'd come back to pick up her phone but actually she'd come back to meet *me*.

As we left the magazine offices, my mobile beeped. I took a quick look. It was Roz *again*.

'You meeting someone?' asked Emily.

I nodded. 'People I'm staying with in Richmond.'

'Oh. You not from London, then?'

'Cornwall. I used to live up in London until just over a year ago. And I'd give anything to come back. I love it up here. It's where it's all happening.'

'So why did you move?'

'Parents split up.'

'Oh, yours too?'

'Why, have yours?'

Emily nodded. 'Two years ago. I live with my mum now. My dad's up in Edinburgh. Hardly see him.'

After that we were off. We found we had so much in common and, as we walked towards the Tube station, I found myself telling her stuff that I hadn't told anyone except Squidge. How much I missed my mates. What I wanted to do in the future. All my plans. She told me all about her books and how she wanted to carry on writing and maybe move to New York and get a huge warehouse flat in Greenwich Village. We found we liked the same music. Liked going to art galleries. As we got close to the Tube station, I didn't want to go.

'It's really easy talking to you,' I said.

'Ditto.' She smiled. 'I'm so glad I went back for my phone. In fact, I thought I knew you when I first saw you but I don't think we have met before, have we?'

'I'd have remembered, believe me,' I said, and I swear she blushed.

'So,' she said, as we saw the sign for Tottenham Court Road, 'here's the Tube station. I guess this is it.'

I checked my watch. I really, really didn't want to go. 'Which way are you going? Maybe we could go together.'

'I was just going to go and hang out along Oxford Street. I've got an hour to kill as I'm going to the theatre later with Mum. I said I'd meet her down here. Shame you have to go, I'd like to talk to you for longer.'

I looked at my watch again. Five o'clock. Roz had arranged for us to go for supper in Richmond later at one of her mates'. She could wait a while. I could say I got caught up with some of the people her dad introduced me to. Not a lie. She didn't need all the details: like I fancied one of them like mad.

'So what are you going to do?' I asked.

'Wander round a few bookshops. Dunno.'

'I'll stay with you. That is . . . if you'd like company?'

Her face lit up. 'I'd love it. But don't you have to be somewhere?'

'I don't have to be back just yet. She can wait.'

'A girl?'

'Mr Williams's daughter. I'm staying with them. I used to know her back in junior school. Haven't seen her for years. Not my girlfriend or anything.'

Emily laughed. 'You don't have to explain yourself to me.'

Oh but I do, I *do,* I thought. I wanted her to know that I was single. Free. Available.

We decided to walk up Oxford Street and window shop and as we headed that way, we got talking again.

'What about you?' I asked trying to sound as casual as I could. 'You attached?'

Emily sighed. 'I was until last week. Michael. We were together for about a year and we've only just split up. Still a bit raw.'

She looked so sad, I wanted to put my arm around her and make her feel better. Inside though, I was thinking, ya*hey*, she's free. Good riddance, Michael, whoever you are.

'Oh, I *am* sorry. Not your decision then?'

'Nope. Out of the blue.'

'He must be mad.'

'You're sweet. I thought we had something really special. We did. He wants to be a writer too. In fact, we met at a creative writing class. It's been hard this past week, I keep trying to work out what I did wrong.'

'Nothing. You couldn't have. This Michael is obviously clinically insane.'

'Don't think he thinks he is.'

'I've just split up with my girlfriend too. It can hit you hard, all right.' I didn't tell her that it was just what I wanted and I wasn't sad at all. I wanted to bond with Emily and thought that if she thought I was in the same situation, she might think we had lot in common and want to spend more time with me, hopefully helping me forget my broken heart.

'What happened?' she asked.

'Oh . . . we wanted different things. You know, same old same old.'

'Yeah. I've been a right mess since it happened. Don't know what to do with myself.'

I sighed. 'Yeah. Me too. It's been good coming up to London. Took my mind off things.' Then I had a moment of inspiration. 'Change of scenery. That's what you need. Come to Cornwall.'

She laughed. 'I've only just met you.'

'So? We might be working together. And . . . I could show you the sights. It is beautiful down there.'

'You've only just been telling me how you can't wait to get back up here.'

'Ah, yes but . . . it's one thing visiting there. Another thing living there all your life. Oh come. It'd be great. How about next weekend? It's a Bank holiday so you could stay a few days. Mum's converted my Gran's house into a B&B

so we have room. At this time of year, we don't have many guests. We can go for long walks. Take in the air. Get over our broken hearts together. Help each other.'

She smiled. 'It's really kind of you to ask me but . . . I think I need some time on my own at the moment. You know, get my head round what's happened with Michael. And . . .' She looked deeply into my eyes causing my insides to melt. 'And you probably need some time on your own too. It's only too easy to get involved on the rebound, before you're ready. You know what I'm saying?'

Damn it, I thought. I know exactly what you're saying. My 'let's bond over our broken hearts' ploy hadn't worked. But I wasn't about to give up.

'I guess you're right, but sometimes . . . well, you have to move on. Make a fresh start.'

'I will. I'm sure I will. I'm just not ready yet. And I'm sure you're not, either.'

I *am*, I thought. I am, I am, I *am*. And with *you*. I didn't say any more though as I didn't want to push her away. That was the last thing I wanted.

'OK. But maybe sometime? I'd love to see you down there.'

Emily stopped and looked at me again. 'You're *so* nice. It's been good meeting you. And it has made me feel better but . . .'

My phone bleeped again. I didn't need to look. I knew it would be Roz. *Bugger* off, I thought.

'Someone's insistent,' said Emily.

And a half, I thought. Just my luck. The one I want doesn't want to get involved. And the one I don't want, does.

Dad

8

I KNEW THE moment that I set foot in Dad's flat on Sunday morning that something was wrong. He looked pale and unshaven, with bloodshot eyes, as if he hadn't slept.

'Looks like you had a rough night,' I said as he let me in and I followed him through to his kitchen at the back.

Dad smiled weakly and went to fill the kettle with water. 'Tea or coffee?'

'Coffee. Thanks. What's up?'

'Nothing. Why? No, I'm fine.'

'So where's Sonia and Tamara?'

Dad switched the kettle on and sat down opposite me at the table. 'Er . . . over at a friend of Sonia's.'

'For lunch?'

Dad shook his head. 'Bit of a row. Nothing we can't sort out. Hungry?' He got up and started rooting round in the fridge. 'Oh. Haven't got much in. The shopping kind of went out of the window yesterday.'

Typical Dad. Not giving anything away. But he did look bad. Troubled. Still, if he didn't want to talk about it, I wasn't going to press him.

'I'm all right, thanks. Had a late breakfast.'

I didn't know what else to say. This was my dad sitting here in front of me. Not a mate like Squidge. What do you say when your dad's had a row with his girlfriend? Discussing our love lives wasn't something we'd ever done much. We talked about art and school, his work. Not personal stuff.

Dad sat back down again. 'So, how's your trip been? Sorry about not being able to give you somewhere to stay. Turns out you could have – Tamara's sleepover got cancelled.'

Must have been a bad row, I thought, as it sounds like Sonia took off yesterday if not before. I decided to give him an opening.

'Women, huh? Sometimes I just don't get them.'

He ran his fingers through his hair. 'Tell me about it. They're another species altogether. Talking of which, how's your mother?'

'OK. Busy as usual. Baking for Britain.'

Dad smiled. 'A force to be reckoned with. She always was.'

We sat there in an awkward silence until the kettle was boiled.

'I'll do it,' I said. 'Coffee or tea?'

'Er . . . tea. Thanks. So . . . how are the Williams family?'

'Also a force to be reckoned with,' I said. 'At least Roz is. I don't know if you remember her.'

I'd had an agonising time with Roz. She had decided yesterday that she was going to give me the green light re coming on to her but I didn't want to. Not that that put her off. As soon as we'd left the safety of her mates after supper last night, she was all over me. I feigned exhaustion but she wasn't having it. In the end, I told her about my 'girlfriend' back in Cornwall. That put her off for a while and at least I was able to get a good night's sleep but she'd clearly rethought the plan overnight. She was very friendly over breakfast, then when she walked me to the Tube to come and see Dad, she'd suddenly pounced on me and given me a huge snog.

'Just in case you ever change your mind,' she'd said when she let me go. 'I wanted to let you know what you're missing.'

If she'd done it twenty-four hours earlier, I might have responded but now I felt nothing. My whole life had changed since then and I knew that there was only one girl for me. And that was Emily.

'So what happened, Dad?' I asked as I placed a mug of tea in front of him.

'Oh. You know. Complicated. She wants commitment. I can't give it to her.'

'Commitment? But how much more committed could you be? She's moved in with you. I would have thought that was pretty permanent.'

Dad didn't say anything. He just gave me a look. At first I didn't get it, then the penny dropped.

'Commitment as in marriage?'

Dad nodded.

'So what did you say?'

Dad looked really uncomfortable and kept moving the mug around the table, as if where he put it was going to make some kind of difference. 'Well, first of all, I wouldn't ever do anything like that without talking to you and Jade.'

Bit late for that, I thought. He didn't consult us when he had the affair.

'But . . . I told her I couldn't do it,' he continued. 'I already have one failed marriage behind me. I don't want another. She said that if that was my attitude then we had no future.'

He looked so sad. I knew he really liked Sonia. And so did I. It took me a while to get my head round him being with her in the beginning and I do still get the occasional twang of jealousy about Tamara being there but she's a kid. She's as mixed up in all this as Jade and I are.

'So what now?' I asked as I wondered if I should give him the 'there are other fish in the sea' line, though it never worked for me. In fact, I always wanted to punch anyone who said it.

'Ball's in her court. I don't want to break up.'

'But you don't want to get married either?'

Dad shook his head, then made an effort to look more cheerful. 'Look, never mind about me. I'm sorry. You just caught me at a bad time. How did the cartoon interview go? What's happening with you?'

I couldn't help but wonder if this might be a good time to broach the subject of me coming back up to London. If Sonia was gone, Tamara was gone, the spare room would be free. Then I felt bad, thinking about myself when he was so obviously distraught.

I began to tell him all about *Kudos* and my interview but I could see that he wasn't really concentrating. I hated seeing him like this. It reminded me of when he and Mum first split up. He looked terrible then. I decided that he needed distracting so I began to talk about a subject I knew would get him going. Our football team (Arsenal). It seemed to do the trick and he shook off his mood to fill me in on the games I'd missed, being down in Cornwall. By the time I had to leave to meet Squidge and Lia, he'd livened up a bit but as I left, I couldn't help but feel that we should have talked more, about what was really going on in both our lives.

'So did you ask your dad about coming back up here?' asked Squidge once we'd settled into our seats for the train journey back.

I shook my head. 'A bit. But it was bad timing. He'd just had a row with Sonia.'

'Oh. Bummer,' said Squidge.

'Looks like they might have split up.'

Lia glanced at Squidge. 'I know this may be an awful thing to say, but . . . maybe you could take Tamara's room.'

'I did think that. Couldn't help it. And as I was leaving, I asked if he'd had time to think about me coming back but, as usual, he gave me a vague answer. The future's unsure, etc., etc.'

'Oh, tough, man,' said Squidge. 'But maybe it will work out.'

'Yeah. But I didn't like seeing him so down. I'll try him another time when things have blown over a bit. But since this visit, I want to get back up here more than ever.'

I was longing to fill Squidge in on the real reason I wanted to live back in London. Emily. But I was afraid that if I told him when Lia was there, she'd tell Cat and Becca and I wasn't sure how Becca would react to me having found the love of my life in less than a week after having broken up with her. I didn't want to hurt her feelings. We started to do homework to pass the time and in between chatted generally about the weekend and what we'd done and I filled them in on my afternoon at the magazine. At last, Lia got up to go to the toilet.

As soon as she'd left the carriage, I leaned over. 'I couldn't tell you before, but it's happened,' I said.

Squidge looked up from his books. 'What's happened?'

'Love! I've fallen in love. The real thing.'

'In love? Ohmigod. She got you.'

'Who got me?'

'Roz.'

'No. Not *Roz.*'

'Then who? Oh no, not Star? I know you've always fancied her but she has a boyfriend and . . .'

'No, not Star. Not Roz. Emily.' Just saying her name made me feel good.

'Who's Emily?' asked Squidge.

'I told you. One of the new faces featuring in the magazine supplement.'

'Oh yeah. The writer?'

'Yeah. I knew the moment I saw her that there was

something special about her. She's really beautiful. I've never felt like this about a girl, ever. And I think she liked me too. We really connected, but she needs some time to get over this jerk who dumped her. Only last week, so she's still a bit raw. Perfect timing, I thought. Anyway . . . now you understand. I need to go back to London to do my A-levels but being with her is pretty high on the agenda too . . .'

Squidge rolled his eyes. 'Talk about fast work.'

'No. Not fast work. It's taken all of my sixteen years to get here. Like I've been waiting all my life for the moment she walked through that door.'

Squidge laughed. 'The Macster in love? You old romantic, you. Told you it would happen one day. Just didn't reckon on it being so soon.'

'Me neither. I feel like all the romantic clichés rolled into one. Love at first sight. Time stood still. Can't stop thinking about her. I felt like I was walking on air when I was with her . . .'

As Lia came back to sit down, I quickly changed the subject and started talking about my dad again.

'It's such a shame your parents split up,' said Lia. 'I couldn't bear it if mine did. And it sounds like your dad isn't very happy.'

'And neither's Mum. In fact . . .' A brilliant idea was beginning to form in my brain.

'What?' asked Squidge.

'No. It's mad, really . . . but . . . I was just thinking something. Mum hasn't moved on. Hasn't met anyone. Not one date even. And Dad's single again and not coping too well by the look of it. When they first broke up, he begged Mum to forgive him. Nah. Forget it. Sorry. Temporary blip of insanity.'

Squidge shrugged and went back to his books and I tried to concentrate on mine as well. But the idea kept popping back into my head.

'Maybe it's not a bad idea . . .'

'What idea?' asked Squidge. 'What are you on about, Mac?'

'Mum and Dad. It's been over a year since they split up. Time heals, so they say. Maybe she's had time to reflect. Maybe she regrets it. In fact, last month I caught her looking at an old album of photos from when we were all together. She looked really sad. And she's always a bit weird when he's phoned or I've been to see him. Like she wants to know all about it and how he is but is shy to ask outright. Do you think . . .? No. Stupid. Although maybe not. No. Yeah. Why didn't I see it before? She might have been acting like that because she wants him back.'

Squidge looked doubtful. 'But your dad? How does he feel about your mum now? He's been with Sonia for a while.'

'Only because Mum wouldn't have anything to do with him. And he did ask about her. And they were together for so long. You can't throw that away, can you?'

Squidge and Lia exchanged anxious looks.

'That's what I'll do,' I said as the plan began to hatch in my head. 'I'll ask Dad to come down to Cornwall. He hasn't been since the break-up and we used to have such great times there when we were kids, staying with Gran. Get him back on the Cornish turf. It's bound to jog his memory about the good times.'

'Hey, Mac,' said Squidge, 'don't get your hopes up. You don't really know what went on.'

'Yes, I do. They had seventeen years of happy marriage. One blip because of that stupid affair and now both of them are unhappy.'

The way was clear. I'd been a fool not to think of it before. I was going to get my parents back together. We could go back and live in London. I'd start dating Emily. And we'd live happily every after.

Sorted.

Women!

9

'**I AM _NOT_ HAVING** that man in this house,' said Mum at supper when I asked if Dad could come to stay.

'I've already asked him,' I said. 'And . . . well, he seemed kind of sad. And he asked after you. And anyway, I phoned him from the train and he said he would try.'

'Try,' said Mum with a sarcastic snort. 'That was his favourite word. You know what it means, don't you? It means maybe, if, might, never. Which is my reply. Never.'

Hmm, I thought, my ploy wasn't working. Need a more 'softly softly' approach. I decided to rethink the plan. Drop things into the conversation over the next week or so to remind her of when things were good between them: memories of Christmases, birthdays, things Dad had done to make her happy. I remembered he used to make her laugh. I'd remind her of those times and she'd be bound to give in. She used to look nice when she laughed. I hadn't seen her like that for a very long time. She's lost a lot of weight since she split up with Dad and most of the time she looks strained. Partly because she puts such long hours in at work, even when she doesn't need to. Maybe she keeps busy so she doesn't have to think about stuff too much.

'Did you get all your homework done?'

'Yes. Did it on the train with Squidge and Lia. We got through loads.'

'Everything ready for school tomorrow?'

'Yes. No. Almost.'

'Right. As soon as supper is finished, up those stairs, lay out what needs ironing then give your room a tidy. It's a tip in there.'

I got up and trudged up the stairs. Welcome home, I thought.

Next on my list was to call Emily and remind her that I existed. We'd swapped numbers before I'd left and promised to get in touch.

'Mac,' she said sounding surprised when I called after supper.

'Hi. Yes. Just wanted to er . . . touch base. See how you were.'

'Oh . . . fine.'

86

She didn't sound fine and she didn't sound as pleased to hear from me as I'd hoped.

'Right. Good. I just wanted to say how much . . .'

'Mac, before you say anything . . . don't . . .'

'Don't? Oh. OK . . .'

'Look, sorry. It was great to meet you on Saturday and . . . well, I talked to Michael yesterday after I'd left you and . . . sorry, I don't want to talk about it. I . . . sorry . . . I did think about you after we'd met but . . .'

But . . . I thought. I hate those buts. I've been thinking about you too, I wanted to say. You've been on my mind every second since we met but I got the feeling that what she wanted to say next was not necessarily what I wanted to hear.

'But . . . do you mind calling back another time? Michael said he'd call this evening and I don't want to miss his call and we still have stuff to talk about.'

'Oh. OK.'

'Thanks. I knew you'd understand, just having broken up with someone as well.'

'What time did he say he'd call? Maybe I could call later.'

'Oh. He just said he'd call Sunday. He might be trying to get through now. So I don't want to stay on the phone too long. So . . . sorry. Catch you another time? Sorry. Bad timing, you know what I mean?'

I felt a sinking feeling in my stomach. Bad timing. It was starting to be the story of my life.

'Sure,' I said. 'That's cool. Bad timing. It happens. Er . . . take care of yourself. OK?'

'Thanks, Mac. I knew you'd understand.'

I don't understand at all, I thought after I'd put the phone down, but I knew I had no choice but to go along with what she wanted. In the meantime, I just hoped that this Michael guy had moved on and wasn't going to make a reappearance in her life. Whatever was happening up there, from the sound of her voice I could tell he was making her unhappy.

'And does Becca know about Roz?' asked Jade when I went down to make a hot chocolate to take to bed with me.

'Know what about Roz? Nothing's going on there, believe me. And anyway, what's it to Becca? We're not an item any more.'

'Just asking,' Jade said with a shrug. 'No need to be defensive.'

'Well, for your information, Miss Nosey Parker, Becca and I are still mates so I *did* tell her that I was staying with Roz.'

'Whatever,' said Jade. 'I've been talking to Dad. He told me what you said about Roz when you went to see him.'

'What?' I said. I'd hardly said anything to Dad, only that Roz was a force to be reckoned with and that I didn't fancy her. 'Anyway, it's none of your business. Why are you taking such an interest?'

'No reason,' she said.

But she was up to something. She had that dangerous look in her eye that she gets when she's hatching a plot.

Roz called my mobile just as I was getting into bed. Luckily, it was on voicemail.

'Just to say what a fabulous weekend I had,' she gushed into the phone, 'and I'm so glad we hooked up again. I can't wait to see you again. And Jade, Jade just phoned actually. She's invited me down and I'd love to come. I've never been to Cornwall and it would be great to see your mum again too. And . . . I . . . I just wanted to say that you don't have to get your sister to invite me, Mac. I know that there's something special between us and – you can invite me yourself. You don't have to be shy and get your sister to do it.'

Arghhhh. Shy! I thought. *Shy?* I'll kill Jade.

On Monday morning, as I checked my e-mails before school, there was an e-card from Roz. *Thinking of you*, it said.

At break, there was a text message: DAD RLY LIKD U. GD LUK WITH UR DRWNGS.

At lunch, another text message: I RLY LKD U2.

'You've got to text her back,' said Squidge when I showed him. 'She's acting like you're having a relationship.'

'And say what?' I asked. 'If I respond, she's going to think I care. If I don't, she's not going to like it.'

'Tell her you want to be friends,' said Squidge. 'And nothing else.'

I knew he was right but somehow I got the feeling that Roz wouldn't be up for doing 'friends'.

God only knows what is going on in Becca's mind. At lunchtime on Monday, she came over to find out how the London trip went. At first she came on all caring-shmaring. Still concerned about having broken my heart (only she hasn't).

She'd heard about Roz on the grapevine (Lia) and what a disaster it had been staying with her, and she tried to be sympathetic. But I could see that she was as smug as anything. Like she believed I couldn't get involved with anyone because I was so devastated about her. It was the perfect time to ask.

'Becca,' I said, 'I need your help.'

'Sure,' she said, 'I'll do anything.'

'OK. You know this girl – Roz?'

'Yeah. She sounds really pushy.'

'Well, that's just it. She wants to come down here. I'm doing everything I can to put her off. But, I have to go along with her to a certain extent as her dad is the magazine editor.'

'Right.'

'So I was wondering if you'd mind if I told her that you're my girlfriend. Just for the time being. Until she gets off my case.'

Becca's look of concern faded fast. 'Say I'm your girlfriend? No *way*. I thought I'd made it clear that I just wanted to be friends from now on.'

'Exactly. I'm asking you as a friend.'

'We have to move on, Mac. *Both* of us. You don't get it, do you?'

Get *what?* I asked myself as she flounced off. Why was she acting so upset? What had I said? She couldn't possibly think I was making up the excuse of needing her to play my girlfriend a bit longer because I didn't want to let go of our relationship. Could she? *Could* she?

I really, really, *really* don't get girls.

On Tuesday morning, a box came in the post with a card and a small cute toy monkey. *This reminded me of you*, said the card and it was signed from Roz with loads of kisses.

* * *

On Tuesday night, I went up to the View café for my cappuccino and to sort out my head and enjoy the sun we'd been having lately. I pulled out my drawing pad and the photos that Mr Williams had given me and did some work on the caricatures. I'd had a few attempts last night but was finding it difficult. Somehow I couldn't let go and draw freely as I knew that Otis, Amanda and Alistair would be insulted if I did. And as for Emily, I couldn't imagine drawing her in any way that didn't flatter her. I stared at her photo and felt angry. Life just wasn't fair. Why did she have to be still involved? Waiting in for some schmuck to call her when he'd obviously moved on? And why did the women who were in my life have to be such a pain in the bum?

I began to sketch a monster with four heads: Mum's, Jade's, Roz's and Becca's, all snarling, ready to eat me up.

The blonde waitress from last week came over to take my order. She glanced at my pad and laughed.

'Still drawing those mad pictures?' she asked.

I put my hand over the page as I hadn't meant anyone to see it.

'No. It's good,' she said. 'You should let people see it. So . . . what's your name?'

'Mac,' I said.

'You go to Torpoint High?'

I nodded.

'I used to go there. Left last year.'

'So what's your name?'

'Sharan. But you can call me Shazza.'

After she'd gone to get my cappuccino, my mobile rang. It was Squidge.

'Just phoning to ask if you want to do that camping thing this weekend?' he said.

'Can't. Got to do these drawings for Roz's dad. But if I get them done, I'll be there.'

'OK. Let me know when.'

'Actually, Squidge, while you're on the phone . . . Girl called Shazza. Blonde. Nice eyes. Big boobs. Do you know her?'

'Works up at the View?'

'Yeah. That's where I am now and she's giving me the eye.'

Squidge laughed. 'She gives everyone the eye. Haven't you got enough on your plate?'

'Nothing that's working,' I replied. 'And Shazza looks like fun.'

'She is,' said Squidge. 'Got a bit of a reputation, in fact. Used to go to our school.'

'I know. So give me the lowdown.'

'Well, I only know what Dan Hall told me after he'd

been out with her. Good-time girl. Likes fun, doesn't like commitment or being tied down. Seems nice though. Easygoing. A laugh.'

Sounds perfect, I thought as I flipped my phone shut.

I decided to try my luck when she came back. Why not? I'm a free man. OK, so she's not Emily but Emily made it very clear that I'm not wanted at the moment. What was I supposed to do? Wait for her? It might take months, years for her to sort things out with Michael. Becca's a headcase who dumped me, so no guilt there. Roz is a control freak and I haven't done anything to lead her on so no guilt there either. Shazza might be just the stop gap I need. Someone to have a laugh with. It wouldn't be love but it wouldn't be complicated. *Just* what I need.

I put on a big smile when she came back a few minutes later with my cappuccino.

'Hey, Shazza . . .'

Looking for a Way Out

10

'YOU CAN'T ACCEPT DEFEAT,' said Squidge. 'It's a cop-out.'

We were sitting in the art room on Thursday night after school. I'd told Mr Barnes all about my chance to work for the magazine and he'd been great – really supportive – and agreed to let me work late in the classroom. It was better than at home, as the desks were bigger and there were no interruptions from Jade being annoying, Mum asking me to do something in the house or Gran trying to recruit me to help on one of her library nights.

I'd spent hours drawing and redrawing the caricatures for Roz's dad. They were rubbish and I was beginning to think it was a big mistake to think I could ever have been a contender.

'But they're not good enough. Surely you can see that?'

Squidge grimaced and flicked through some of my other

drawings in my portfolio. 'It's hard to say, Mac. These other ones that you've done of your mum and Jade and Becca and Roz, they're brilliant. They have an edge. Like you'd totally let go when you did them. Didn't think about whether they were good or not, you drew what you felt.'

'Only because I thought no one would ever see them. They're not for public consumption.'

'So you're trying to draw what you think people want to see?'

'Sort of.'

'That's a killer in any kind of artform, you know that. It has to be raw. You have to tell the truth about what you feel.'

'I know. And that's why the drawings are lukewarm. I don't feel *anything*. I hardly know these guys. I can't let go and draw something beyond my first impression of them. They were OK people so that's how the drawings are coming out. OK, but nothing more.'

'You can't give up,' said Squidge. 'I won't let you. The other drawings show that you can do it. Find out more about them. Their dark sides or something and then let go of trying to please.'

I knew what he meant but it wasn't happening. I'm a people-pleaser by nature. Don't upset the boat. Don't confront. That's me. Not the best qualities for a caricaturist. And no way would I get the gig if I sent in the half-hearted attempts that I'd done so far.

'At least I've learnt how hard it is,' I said, sighing. 'It's one thing doing your own private work. Another doing a professional brief and going public.'

'Hi, guys,' said Becca appearing at the door. 'You in here again?'

She came over to look at what I was doing. I quickly hid the drawing of her as one of the four heads of my monster.

'Yeah, still trying to do these drawings for the magazine, but they're not working out.'

She flicked through a few at the top then looked at Squidge.

'Er, can I have a private moment with Mac, Squidge?'

'Sure,' he said. 'Catch you later.'

Oh no, don't leave, I tried to say to him telepathically but sadly my psychic skills were like my artistic ones – useless – and a moment later, he'd disappeared out of the room.

Becca sat down opposite. 'I've reconsidered your request,' she said. 'Squidge told Lia that Roz has been bugging you all the time with texts and phone calls and acting like she's your girlfriend so I've decided to help. If you want to say that we're still an item, then go ahead. I'll play along. I want you to know that I'm here for you.'

I carefully scrutinised her face to see if there was any hidden agenda but no, she seemed to be on the level.

'Right. OK. Thanks.'

'No problem,' she said, then got up. 'That's what friends are for. I know this cartooning thing means a lot to you and I want to help. So how's it going?'

'To tell the truth, I'm thinking of backing out. I should have something ready to send by now but my drawings just aren't good enough.'

'Let's have a proper look.'

I handed her a pile I'd done of Otis, Amanda and Alistair. I kept the one of Emily to myself as I didn't want Becca asking about her – she'd suss me out in no time, especially as I'd drawn a big heart round her.

Becca glanced through. 'I think these are OK . . .'

'That's it. *OK*. No one wants OK. OK is mediocre. They want brilliant.'

'You can do it, Mac. I know you can. So, these aren't your best work. But I've seen the one of your gran and that's brilliant. And I've seen the one of your family as the witches in *Macbeth* and that's brilliant. So I *know* you can do it. You can't give up, Mac. Not now. You can't.'

'That's what Squidge said. But I know I'm not cutting the mustard.'

'I felt like that loads of times when I went in for that Pop

Princess competition. *Loads* of times. Giving up isn't the answer. You'll regret it. I know you will. It's your dream to be a cartoonist and if you back out at the first hurdle, you'll never get anywhere. I remember when I felt like giving up at one point in the competition, I saw a quote that my dad had in his office. "No failure except in not trying," it said. You've at least got to try, give it your best shot.'

'You don't understand. I have tried and my drawings are crap.'

'Then do some more. I believe in you.'

So many people were behind me. It only made it worse. Mr Barnes was being great. Squidge was being great and now Becca was being great. Gran. Mum. All of them saying how much they believed in me, but I knew the truth. That I was a failure. And I felt lousy that I was going to let them all down.

When Becca had gone, I did have another go. I tried letting go and giving myself permission to just draw but still all that came out was bland, bland, bland. Nice sketches of four *nice* people. That's not what they were about and apart from Alistair, they deserved better. In the end, I drew a team of cheerleaders: Squidge, Becca and Mr Barnes in a line with little ra-ra skirts on and T-shirts saying 'Mac', then me bent over with exhaustion, looking weedy and knock-kneed on a racetrack coming last in a race. After an hour or so, the school caretaker came round to lock up, so I got up to go.

Squidge and Becca didn't understand. I wasn't good enough. As I made my way out towards the bus stop, I racked my brains for a way of bowing out gracefully and without making them feel like I'd let them down.

Back at home, Mum was listening to Radio 4 in the kitchen. I didn't feel like talking much so I sat and listened with her as I ate my supper. It was some book programme and an author was talking about the stress of meeting deadlines.

'Once, I actually considered breaking my arm,' the author said, 'so that I had a good excuse not to finish on time.'

The author and the interviewer laughed, but I didn't. She'd given me my get out.

At nine o'clock, when Roz phoned for her nightly chat, I was ready for her.

'So how's it going?'

'Oh Roz, hi,' I said. 'I'm so glad you phoned, I was going to call you but I've just got back from the doctor's. I . . . I've had a bit of an accident.'

'Ohmigod! Are you all right?'

'Yes. Bit shaken. But I'm afraid I've broken my wrist. Such a bummer. I can't use my hand.'

'Which hand?'

'My left one. My drawing one. I'm so sorry to have let you down like this but it will be weeks before I can use it again. Please can you explain to your dad. I feel really bad about this but I can't even pick up a pencil, so there's no way I can draw.'

'Oh, Mac,' said Roz. 'I'm *so* sorry. You poor thing. That's just so unfair. What happened?'

'Oh . . . um . . . bike. Someone drove in front of me and I had to swerve and I hit the side of the kerb and came straight off.'

'I *so* wish I was there and could kiss it better.'

'Thanks, Roz. I'll be OK. Anyway, got to go. Bit tired. Shock and all that. Look. I'll be in touch and thanks for everything.'

And that was the end of that, I thought as I put the phone down a minute later. I felt bad about lying to her but it was my only way out without losing face. Probably for the best, I thought as I trudged upstairs. Better than submitting work and having it rejected.

Half an hour later, as I was doing my homework and listening to a CD that Squidge had lent me, Jade burst into my room.

'What?' I asked.

'Nothing,' she said. 'Er . . . can I borrow a pen?'

'Sure. Over on the desk,' I said and went back to my work.

Ten minutes later, the phone rang downstairs.

'For you, Mac,' Gran called up the stairs.

I went down and picked up the receiver.

'Mac, it's me,' said Roz in a sad voice.

I sighed. I thought I'd finally got rid of her.

'I called Jade after we'd spoken, as I was afraid that you were putting on a brave face about your accident. I wanted to know how you really were. She didn't seem to know anything about your hand. And . . . she just called me back . . .'

Bugger, I thought as Jade appeared at the top of the stairs, held her wrist as though it was painful and stuck her tongue out.

'Ah . . . yes . . . I can explain . . .'

'You don't have to,' she said. 'I understand.'

'You do?'

'Yes. You wanted to get out of the cartooning job.'

'How did you know?'

'Silly. I *know* you. I could hear it in your voice earlier in the week. I could tell that you were having doubts about your drawings.'

'That's it exactly, Roz. They're not good enough and I

didn't want to let you down. I thought this way . . .'

'Silly boy. But no, Mac, it's not an option. I know that you lack confidence. I knew that when you got Jade to call and ask me to come and visit. And I could tell by the way you were so nervous when you were up in London. But I think it's so sweet. I hate people who are full of themselves and you being a bit shy is one of the reasons I like you so much. Like you don't realise how attractive you are, and you don't realise how talented you are. It's so common with artists. They aren't good at selling themselves and that's why they have agents to do it for them. That's what you need. An agent. Do some copies of what you've done so far and let me have a look.'

I couldn't believe it. I'd blatantly lied and she was acting all motherly and understanding. I *really* don't get women, more than ever.

'Oh, right. Is that what I need?'

'Yes. Someone who is there for you, who really understands and cares for you . . .'

I had a feeling that I knew what was coming next.

'Someone like me . . .'

11

Phone Crazy

'*TOOOOOM*,' yelled Jade. 'It's for you *again* . . .'

I got up from my desk to go downstairs. Roz had only just phoned but knowing her, she'd probably worked out a game plan for the rest of my life in the last ten minutes.

'Who is it?' I asked as I reached the hall.

Jade shrugged. 'Dunno. I'm not your secretary.'

I took the receiver from her and I felt my chest tighten when I heard the voice at the other end.

'Mac. It's Emily. I hope you don't mind me calling so late but I had to speak to you.'

'No. Course not. How are you?'

'Good. Well, better than I was. I've been doing a lot of thinking this week and . . . well, I wondered if your offer was still open.'

'What, to come down here?'

'Yes. One of my friends is driving down to Penzance with her parents on Saturday and said that they could give me a lift. I asked Mum and she said I could go if she can speak to your mum at some point. It seemed to be . . . I don't know, sounds silly, but too good an opportunity to miss . . .'

'Not silly at all. Wow . . . so . . . but what made you change your mind?'

'Oh, lots of things. Mainly, that I've been a complete idiot. I can see that now. I waited all week for Michael to call, going mental. I've been such a fool sitting in, waiting for a call that never came and I realised that you were right. I need to move on. Make a fresh start – and I can't do that up here at the moment, always watching the phone, willing it to ring. I can't bear another second here. So change of air. New experiences. No stupid phone to stare at all night.'

'I . . . no, wow, that will be brilliant. Let me just ask Mum.'

I quickly put the phone down and ran to find Mum. She was in the living room with Gran, watching TV.

'Mum, can a friend stay this weekend? One of the people from the magazine? The writer girl. Emily. She's passing through. It will help with my drawings. And will you OK it with her mum some time so that she knows I'm not a mad person?'

Mum glanced at Gran and she nodded. 'Sure. We haven't got any other guests booked in so far, though I'm still hoping. She can have the blue room unless we get a coach load of rich Americans booking in at the last minute.'

Not much chance of that, I thought as I raced back to the phone and told Emily the good news. I felt like dancing round the house. Squidge and Becca had been right. Don't give up. Don't give up.

I went back up to my room, taking the stairs two at a time and almost knocked Jade over as she was lurking at the top of the stairs.

'You look happy,' she said.

'I am,' I said. 'Lesson one in life Jade. Never give up.'

'Humpf,' she said and flounced into her room.

I spent all day Friday daydreaming about where I'd take Emily, the sights I thought she'd enjoy the most.

'Earth to planet Mac,' said Squidge as we rode home on the bus after school. 'Earth to planet Mac.'

I laughed. 'Bank Holiday weekend. Three whole days off and Emily for company. The forecast is for more early summer sun. It couldn't be more brilliant. Even Jade's being cool about it. Apparently, she knows Emily's book and likes the idea of having a celeb in the house. Something to show off about to all her friends.'

'Typical,' said Squidge. 'But I thought we were going to go camping.'

'Oh. Sorry. Yeah. Can we do it another time?'

'Sure . . . but what about Shazza? I thought you were going to be seeing her.'

'Oh!' I'd forgotten about her. 'Oh, no worries. I said I'd give her a call. We didn't have anything definite planned. And you said she wasn't into heavy commitments. I'm sure she'll understand.'

'Well, I hope it all works out for you,' said Squidge.

'Oh, it will, it will. I've got a feeling things are going to go my way for a while.'

When I got home, I helped Mum change the bedlinen in the blue room and picked some roses from the garden to put by Emily's bed.

Mum smiled. 'Seems you like this girl?'

Normally I didn't like to discuss my love life with Mum, but it was hard not to, seeing as Emily was going to be staying under the same roof.

'Early days,' I said. 'But she did seem . . . well, kind of special.'

Mum smiled again. 'Oh, and Mac . . .' she said as she plumped up the pillows, 'I've been thinking about your dad. What you said. If it really means so much to you, I won't object to him coming. I . . . I know I can seem a bit harsh sometimes but . . . well . . . I know he's still your father and it's important that he's involved in your life down here.'

I gave her a huge hug. Women, I thought. They don't half change their minds a lot. First Becca, then Emily and now my mum. I must remember this for the future. That no matter how fixed they are about something, give them a bit of time and they'll do a total turnaround.

At nine o'clock on the dot, Roz phoned. She'd been with her dad along to the meeting with the new faces and the prospective cartoonists.

'As your agent,' she said, 'I thought I should be there to represent you. And I got the copies you sent of what you've done so far and I know what you mean. They're almost there. You can do it. I know you can.'

For a moment, my stomach lurched. I didn't care what she thought of my rubbish caricature attempts. She'd have seen Emily. I hoped she hadn't said anything about coming down tomorrow.

I didn't have to wait too long to find out as almost as soon as I put down the phone to Roz, Emily called. She sounded strange.

'So give me a call when you're getting close,' I said, 'and I'll arrange where to meet you.'

Silence at the other end.

'What? Emily, what is it?'

'Roz,' she said.

'What about Roz?'

'She was at the meeting.'

'I know. She just phoned. She . . . Did you tell her you were coming down?'

'No. But she told Otis what was going on with you two.'

'Going on with us? Nothing's going on . . .'

'Not what she said to Otis. She said you'd invited her down to Cornwall.'

'Roz? No way. It was my sister who invited her down.'

'She said that you two had something really special going and that although it wasn't working for a while, now you're on track. Oh Mac, why didn't you tell me it was her.'

'Her? No. What do you mean?'

'That it was Roz that you broke up with. And now it seems you've got back together.'

'What! No. Roz is *not* my girlfriend. My girlfriend is Becca. No. I mean, was. She isn't any more. Becca, that is. And neither is Roz. I was just staying with her. I told you. Mr Williams's daughter. The one who was calling me all the time when we were together. I told you then that she wasn't my girlfriend. *Remember?* You said I didn't have to explain myself to you. But honestly, there's nothing going on between us.'

I could hear Emily sigh heavily at the other end of the

phone. 'Sounds to me like you have a lot to work out, Mac. I don't think this would be a good time for me to come down. So that's why I'm phoning, to tell you that I won't be coming after all.'

'*No* . . .' I objected into the phone but it was too late. She'd hung up.

As always, Jade was hovering in a doorway listening in. She must have seen my face fall.

'Bad news?' she asked.

'The worst.'

'Why?'

'Emily's not coming. She thinks that Roz is my girlfriend.'

'That's the impression I got from talking to Roz. She's really into you, you know.'

'Well, it's not mutual and now she's messed everything up.'

I sat on the bottom of the stairs and put my head in my hands.

Jade sat down next to me and put her hand lightly on my back.

'What was it you were telling me last night? Lesson one in life. Never give up. So sort it. Get back on the phone and tell Emily the truth.' She gave me a gentle shove. 'Go on. Do it. Nothing ever happens unless you make it.'

Jade being nice to me? What the hell was going on? But she was right. I got up, went back to the phone and dialled Emily's number.

She picked up straight away and for a second I hoped that my call wasn't going to be a disappointment and that she was still expecting Michael.

'Emily,' I said, 'please listen. Please come. I really want you to. No . . . Before you say anything, let me put a few things straight for you. Becca – Becca was my girlfriend down here. She's the one I told you about. We broke up before I came up to London. That's over. Roz – Roz is Mr Williams's daughter. I've known her since she was little. She always had a crush on me which, by the way, was never reciprocated. That must be what she meant by saying that we didn't get off to a good start. I saw her for the first time in years last weekend and she . . . well . . . nothing is going on. *Nothing*. Really. It's all in her head. Nothing has happened – will happen. I'm not into her at all but she doesn't seem to have got the message. I've given her no reason to think that what she feels is mutual. Please don't let her ruin things for us. Please come down. I'm being totally honest with you. It's you I want to spend time with. Only you.'

There was a silence at the other end. 'OK,' she said. 'See you Saturday.'

'Well done,' said Jade when I'd put the phone down. 'I was *dreading* having to tell my friends that she didn't come after all.'

Hmm, I thought. I might have known she'd have had some hidden agenda. But I didn't mind. If it hadn't been for her I wouldn't have made the call. Good old Jade. Sometimes she could be all right.

Emily's Visit

12

'OH MUM, does Jade *have* to come?' I groaned.

'You'll have plenty of time on your own with Emily later,' said Mum on Saturday afternoon as she went out to the car to go and meet Emily.

Mum had agreed to go and fetch her, as she was being dropped off at a pub up near the A38 so that her friend and her parents could carry on down the road to Penzance. Better than bringing her back on the bus, I thought, but Jade had insisted that she wanted to come with us. Not part of my plan, I thought. I mean, who wants your mum and your sister along when you're going to meet the love of your life? I had the whole weekend worked out in my head. Bring her back to the house. Settle in. Go for long walks. Show her the area. Just the two of us, getting to know each other better.

In the end, it wasn't a bad thing that Jade came along. When we met Emily, something strange happened to my vocal cords and all the witty and interesting things I had planned to say went straight out of the window. She was even lovelier than I remembered, dressed in white jeans and a white Indian top. Jade was straight in there as soon as we got back in the car, asking about her books and her writing and what was happening in London. I sat in the back listening and gazing at her profile in the front when I thought no one was looking. At one point Mum caught me and winked in the rear-view mirror. Relax, I told myself, I'd soon have her alone and then we could talk properly without an audience listening in. I'd take her for a walk down at Mount Edgecumbe as soon as we'd got home and she'd unpacked.

'Would you like to see the area?' asked Mum as we drove back towards the peninsula.

'I'd love to,' said Emily. 'I've never been here before so I want to see as much as I can.'

Noooo, I thought. *I* want to be the tour guide. Introduce her to my special places, see her face when she looks out over some of the glorious views. I want her to remember it as being *me* who showed her all the beauty spots.

'It's OK, Mum. I can take her round. Let's get home.'

'Don't be silly, Mac. You know that you can see more

by car in the first instance. Let's have a drive round so that Emily can get a feel for the place and then you can decide where you want to go and look at more closely after that.'

I felt like going into a ginormous sulk but knew that it wouldn't look good. Petulant adolescent is not a great way to impress a girl, so I had to agree.

'OK. But take the coast road so that she can get the view there. It's always spectacular every time you see it.'

And so we spent the first hour crammed in the car being chauffeured and chaperoned – Mum acting as our tour guide and Jade jabbering on from the back – as we took the road along Whitsand Bay up to Rame and then down into the villages of Kingsand and Cawsand where we had a short walk so that she could see the beaches there.

Emily was well impressed and oohed and aahed in all the right places and it was fun showing someone new all the sights. It was like seeing it for the first time again myself.

'I *love* this place,' she said as we sat for a moment (with Jade between us) on the wall by the beach at Cawsand Bay. 'It's so unspoilt and so . . .' She sniffed the air. 'It smells so clean. Such a change from the traffic fumes in London.'

'You must be tired after your journey,' said Mum. 'How about a cup of tea or something?'

'That would be lovely,' said Emily, turning to me.

'Where's that café you like, Mac? The one you told me about, where you go after school?'

'Oh,' I said as panic seized me. She meant the View. I couldn't take her there. What if Shazza was there and she asked if I was going to take her out as arranged? Hell no. That would ruin everything. 'Café. Yes. Right. Down in Kingsand Bay. On the front. We just have to walk through the village. About ten minutes.'

Emily looked puzzled. 'In the bay? No. I distinctly got the impression it was up high somewhere as you spoke about the view from there. Remember? Only sky and sea as far as the eye can see, you said.'

'You mean the View,' said Jade. 'That's up at Whitsand.'

'The View. That was it,' said Emily. 'Is it far?'

'Actually, we drove past it before,' I lied. 'It closes at four at the weekends.'

'Does not,' said Jade. 'I've often been up there in the early evening.'

Remind me to kill you, I thought as my mind went into overdrive imagining embarrassing scenes with Shazza.

'Would you like to go?' asked Jade, digging my grave even deeper.

Nooooooooooooooo, I prayed. Please God, no. Don't ruin everything now. Please, please.

'You've got all weekend,' said Mum, getting up from the

wall and getting her car keys out. 'Why don't we take you home, you can settle in and go up there tomorrow? We can have a cup of tea at home.'

Oh, thank you, God, I thought. Thank you, thank you. I wanted to hug Mum. I'd find something else to do tomorrow and make sure we went nowhere near the View.

'And Mum does do the best cakes in the area,' said Jade as we headed back for the car.

Saved by the bell, I thought as I settled in the back and planned the rest of the day. All I wanted to do was get her alone.

Gran opened the front door and came out to meet us as soon as the car drew up in front of the house. She looked really smart in a navy blue shirt, trousers and a blue bead necklace. Where was she going? I wondered. She rarely dressed up these days.

Sadly, she wasn't going anywhere. She was waiting for Emily.

'I'm so pleased to meet you,' she gushed as soon as Emily was out of the car and had been introduced. 'I thought you'd be back ages ago.'

'Mum drove us round the area,' I explained. 'And now . . .'

'I hope you don't mind, dear,' said Gran to Emily, 'but I

have a few people who are dying to meet you. You see, I work at the library and on a Thursday night, they hold a creative writing class. When the girls heard that we had a real author coming, well, they begged me to let them come and meet you. And we all know your book, we have it in the library. It's very popular with the teens.'

I glanced over at the house and saw the 'girls' all standing expectantly at the window. White haired every one of them and not one under sixty. Mrs Marshall from the co-op gave us a wave.

'Gosh,' said Emily. 'I'd hardly call myself a real author. I've only done one book so far, but that's so sweet of you.'

'And Emily's only just arrived,' I said. 'She probably needs to rest.'

'No. I don't mind,' said Emily. 'I love meeting other writers and talking books.'

'I'll go and fix you some tea then and bring it through,' said Mum.

'And can I sit in?' asked Jade. 'I like talking books as well.'

Yeah right, I thought. The last book I'd seen Jade reading was *Harry Potter* when she was nine and she didn't finish that. She only wanted to sit in so that she could show off to her friends about spending time with a London author.

So much for my great plans to be alone with Emily in some romantic location, I thought later as I sat taking tea with five old dears, Emily, my mum and Jade. Once again, my destiny seemed to have been taken over by women.

The 'literary salon' went on for hours as Gran's ladies had a million and one questions to ask Emily. Where did she get her ideas? How long did it take to write a book? What did she like to read? How did she work out her plots? Create her characters? And it was interesting to sit in the corner of the room and hear Emily talk about what was clearly her passion. She didn't seem to mind having been hijacked to talk to them at all.

When it got to early evening, there was no sign of the session wrapping up and Gran's ladies were still hanging about as Mum began preparing supper. In the end, she asked if they'd like to stay. I felt myself inwardly groan. It seemed like I was never going to get Emily alone.

'There's always tomorrow,' said Mum with a wink as I helped her set the table in the kitchen.

'I hope so,' I said. 'She's my guest. Not theirs.'

Mum laughed. 'The course of true love never did run smooth.'

'Tell me about it,' I said, sighing.

* * *

Sunday morning and not a cloud in the sky. I was up bright and early, ready to take Emily out. Jade was still in bed, Gran had already set off on one of her walks and Mum was busy in the kitchen preparing some of her wares for Cat's dad's shop the next morning. At last, I was going to be able to spend time with Emily.

'I'm so sorry about all the distractions yesterday,' I said when she appeared at around nine.

'No problem,' she said. 'I like to go with the flow sometimes, but I'm looking forward to today. I'd hoped you could show me around a bit.'

At last, we were back on course, I thought, as we had breakfast then set off for the gardens down at Mount Edgecumbe. As we took the back path through the fields to Cremyl, we soon fell back into chatting easily and enjoying each other's company. I showed her the Italian gardens, we had coffee in the Orangery, walked along the sea wall and looked out over at Plymouth and all the boats moored there.

'I could live here,' said Emily. 'Maybe when I'm rich, I'll buy a house and come down here for the summers. It would be a great place to write. Did you know that Daphne Du Maurier lived down here some place? I love her books.'

'She lived further down, in Fowey,' I said, as images of us together in a picturesque cottage floated through my mind. We could have a summer place in Cornwall and a pad up in

London for the winter. She could do her books, I'd do my cartoons and everyone would invite us to glamorous parties with loads of creative people. It would be brilliant.

After an hour or so of exploring the gardens, Emily turned to me. 'I'm starving,' she said. 'Must be this sea air. How about we go to that café of yours now?'

'Oh. Right. No. It's miles away up there. And it might not be open.'

'Oh, come on, let's give it a shot. Isn't there a bus or something? How do you get there?'

'Bus on the way home from school.'

'So it must go from Cremyl, yes? Where the foot ferry comes in?'

'Yes, but er . . .'

She took my hand and pulled me back towards Cremyl. It was the first time we'd held hands and I felt a volt of electricity course through me when she put her hand in mine. I'd been thinking about doing it all morning but didn't want to freak her out, in case she was still not over Michael but she did it so naturally and now there we were walking along hand in hand. I felt as if I was floating on air.

At the bus stop, I prayed that God would intervene again and prevent us getting up to the café. The bus would break down. The drivers would be on strike. I didn't want anything to break the mood that we were in.

'Are you sure you want to go up there?' I tried again. 'We can get a snack and a coffee in the pub here.'

'But it was beautiful up there when we drove past yesterday. And it's such a lovely day. Oh please, let's go.'

'OK, but I thought we could go there tomorrow and . . . I had a few places in mind to show you this afternoon.' I knew that the café was definitely closed on a Monday so it wouldn't be a problem.

'Oh, let's go now,' she said and began to snuggle in to me, putting one arm round my waist and her other arm around my shoulder. I looked down at her and she looked up at me, an amazing moment when it felt like time stood still. I'd never felt so good as she turned her face up towards mine so that I could kiss her. Just as I was leaning in and about to touch her lips with mine, I heard a familiar voice.

'Hey, Mac.'

Emily and I sprang apart. It was Becca, standing right in front of us with her hands on her hips and she didn't look very happy.

'Oh . . . Becca, this is . . .'

'I think I know *exactly* who this is,' said Becca. 'And I'd like to know what she's doing cuddling up to *my* boyfriend.'

Emily looked totally bewildered. 'Becca. No, it's all right. I . . .'

'No. It's not all right,' she said, then she started sobbing.

'I thought I could trust you, Mac. I thought you . . . we . . . How *could* you?'

Emily looked aghast. 'I'm so sorry. Mac told me it was over with you.'

'Over? *Over*? Not at all,' sobbed Becca.

Emily gave me a withering look then turned back to Becca who was mid-sob. 'Oh, Becca. I . . . I would never have . . . Oh, Mac!'

She turned and ran back down the path through the field towards our house.

'What the hell do you think you're playing at?' I yelled at Becca.

Becca turned off the waterworks straight away and grinned. 'Good, wasn't I? Very convincing. Think it did the trick.'

'I'll say. But why would you do that? Are you *mad*?"

Becca's face flushed red. 'You asked me to,' she said angrily. 'I was doing what *you* asked. Helping you get rid of Roz.'

'Only that's NOT Roz. That's Emily.'

'Jesus,' said Becca, looking confused. 'Who's Emily?'

'Oh, never mind,' I said as I took off down the path after Emily.

'Never mind yourself,' said Becca after me. 'I was *trying* to help for God's sake. I thought that's what you wanted.'

And off she flounced in a huff.

I ran as fast as I could but Emily still got back before me.

'What's going on?' asked Mum, as I sped past her up the stairs.

'Nothing,' I said and took the stairs two at a time.

Upstairs, Emily had locked her door. I knocked gently.

'Emily, let me in.'

'Go away.'

'But this is ridiculous. I can explain.'

Emily opened the door. 'Like you explained about Roz. Seems to me that you have a string of girls all thinking that they're your girlfriend. Well, I can tell you now, I'm not going to be one of them. I like boys who are honest. And clear.'

'Look, let me come in. Let's talk.'

'Talk all you want. I've called a taxi to take me to the station. It's coming any minute,' she said as she went back into her room and stuffed her clothes into her bag.

'But it's three hours back to London. And there were so many places I wanted to show you.'

'Show them to your other girlfriends, Mac. I won't be messed around like this.'

At that moment, a car beeped outside. Emily went to the window and looked out.

'That will be my taxi,' she said, then picked up her bag

and walked past me. 'Excuse me.'

I followed her downstairs. 'No, really, Emily. Please. Give me a chance. Let me explain, at least.'

At the foot of the stairs, she turned to me, her expression completely cold. 'Say thanks to your mum and your gran. Oh and Jade. It was nice meeting them.'

And with that, she went out the front door, got into the taxi and was driven away.

13 Fantasy Girl

I WENT BACK UP to my room and locked the door. Life just isn't fair, I thought as I paced up and down. I felt in complete turmoil. Should I follow her to the station? Should I call her? Should I throw myself off the nearest bridge? Women. There's no pleasing them. Why hadn't she given me a chance? I could have explained. But then how would it have sounded? I'd asked my ex-girlfriend to lie and pretend we were still an item to put Roz off. It sounded cowardly, that's how it sounded. Maybe it was a good thing I hadn't tried to explain. Oh hell, oh hell, oh hell. I felt angry. With myself, with Emily, with Becca, with everyone. I just couldn't win, no matter what I did and now Emily thought I was a love rat with a string of girlfriends.

I tried Emily's mobile but as expected, it was on voicemail. I didn't leave a message. She probably wouldn't listen to it if she thought it was me.

I lay on the bed and listened to some music but no matter how loud I turned it up, it wouldn't drown out my thoughts.

Mum kept knocking on my door so after a while, I let her in. 'What was all that about?' she asked.

'Big misunderstanding.'

'But what could have possibly happened? You were getting on so well before.'

'Don't want to talk about it.'

Mum sat on the end of the bed. 'Mac, you can talk to me. You didn't . . . did you try to get Emily to do something she didn't want to do?'

'*Muuuum*. No! I wouldn't do that. What do you think I am?' I couldn't believe she would even think such a thing.

'A sixteen-year-old boy. I remember how carried away they used to get in my day.'

'*Muuum* . . .'

'So what happened? Emily seemed so upset when she came in.'

'Becca. Becca only went and pretended that she was still my girlfriend.'

'But . . . I thought it was over with you two?'

'It is.'

'So why on earth would she pretend to still be your girlfriend?'

127

'Ah . . .' No way could I explain that. 'Look, Mum. I just need some time alone. Please. It was just a big misunderstanding about something.'

Mum got up. 'If that's what you want but . . . I'd like to help.'

'Thanks, Mum,' I said as she left the room. My whole life is a mess, I thought as I lay back on the bed. Outside the sun is shining but in here, there's only gloom.

I caught sight of my miserable reflection in the mirror on the back of the door. 'Oh, get a life,' I told myself.

I went over to my desk and tried to do some drawings. After a few half-hearted attempts, I gave up. That definitely wasn't happening. What could I do with myself? I hated feeling like this and soon Jade would be around and then Gran. No doubt they would want all the sordid details about why Emily left. I had to get out and fast.

I rang Squidge's number but like Emily's, it was on voicemail. He was probably out some place with Lia. Where could I go? Somewhere to take my mind off all of this? There must be someone or some place to distract me, I thought, otherwise I'm going to lose my mind. Suddenly I had an idea. Should I? Shouldn't I? Oh, to hell with it, I thought as I reached for the phone.

* * *

'Hey, Mac, I'm so glad you called,' said Shazza. 'I was hoping you would. Want to come over? I was just sitting here in the garden catching some sun and reading some mags. Come over and hang out. My parents are out for the day so we'll have the place to ourselves.'

'I'll be there as soon as I can,' I said and took down the directions she gave me. She lived in a remote part of the peninsula, slightly off the bus route – but why not? I thought. I'm a free man. She's a free woman and she might take my mind off things for the afternoon.

The bus service on a Sunday is slow and when I got down to Cremyl, it looked like the one that left for near where Shazza lived had just gone. It would be two hours before the next one arrived so I decided to walk. The fresh air might clear my head, I thought as I set off up the road.

It took an hour and a half to get there but I made it. Up a dirt track and there it was, an old farm house with barns out the back. By the time I got there, I was sweltering as it was a hot day with not a cloud in the sky.

Shazza answered the door in a tiny turquoise bikini. I felt myself blush as she has an amazing body. It was hard not to look at her boobs, as they were just about falling out of her bikini top.

'Fab day, isn't it?' she said as she motioned me to follow her. She led me through the house and into the back garden where there were a couple of deck chairs and she'd laid out a blanket on the lawn. 'Take your T-shirt off. Get comfortable. Do you want a pair of shorts?'

'Er, no. Thanks,' I said as I stripped off my T-shirt. 'I'm fine.' Actually I was still boiling but I wasn't taking off my jeans. My legs were still lily white from the winter.

Shazza, on the other hand, had no inhibitions and lay on the blanket and stripped off her bikini top. My eyes almost fell out of my head. This was proving to be a lot more of a distraction that I'd imagined. Woah, wahey, I thought. My first glimpse of an almost naked girl. Maybe it was going to turn out to be my lucky day after all.

'You don't mind, do you?' she said as she tucked her top under the blanket. 'Only I hate getting sun marks. It looks so naff and I'm sure I haven't got anything you haven't seen before.'

'Oh! No. You go ahead. No. Fine. Lovely.' Oh shut up, Mac, I thought. Stop acting like the village idiot and stop staring at her boobs.

I tried to adopt a 'man of the world' type stance and look cool as Shazza motioned for me to sit down next to her then picked up a bottle of sun tan lotion.

'You're pretty white,' she said looking at my chest. 'Here. Lie down and I'll put some lotion on you.'

Holy Moley, if Squidge could see me now, I thought, as

I lay down and she began to apply lotion to my chest and arms. I was glad I'd kept my jeans on – the sight of Shazza with no top on and then kneeling over me was having quite an effect. Mainly in the trouser department. I hoped that Shazza hadn't noticed that my jeans now had an embarrassing lump in them. Squidge calls it Polonius Plonker. Always standing to attention at inappropriate moments. And my old Polonius certainly was now.

After she'd applied the lotion, we lay in the sun and chatted and Shazza told me all about how she wanted to train to be a beauty therapist and move to Plymouth or Bristol. It was strange. It was relaxing as I wasn't doing anything but lying in the sun with a half naked girl but I also felt incredibly tense. Get a grip, I kept told myself. This was the kind of moment I'd been dreaming of as Shazza was like a fantasy babe who'd stepped off the pages of one the magazines I'm not supposed to have.

After an hour or so, Shazza went in to get some juice. Life is strange, I thought, as she brought the tray out to us. You really don't know what's around the corner. Only this morning, I was walking in the woods with Emily, worried about holding her hand and now here I am with my very own Page Three girl, bouncing towards me as I lie here in her garden.

Shazza lay down on the blanket next to me, *close* next to

me, so that our thighs were touching, and looked at me coyly. So many times, I'd got the signals wrong in the past but it seemed to me that she was definitely giving me the come on. I shifted over and put my arm around her. She snuggled in. The feel of her skin against mine felt incredible. It was like silk. Oo-er, there goes Polonius Plonker again, I thought, as I felt a stirring in my jeans. But wow, this is definitely my lucky day! I liked Shazza. She was everything that Squidge had said. Easygoing. Made you feel comfortable. And she knows exactly what she wants and isn't afraid to go for it.

Five minutes later, we were snogging. It felt amazing – sun shining down on us, her in my arms all oily from the lotion, the lemony scent of her hair. And she didn't seem to mind where I put my hands. Any moment now and I was going to get my first feel of a girl's breasts. I began to feel that I'd died and gone to heaven.

And then suddenly Shazza let out a sob, turned away, sat up and burst into tears.

Crumbling crustaceans! I thought as I sat up with her.

'What?' I asked. 'What did I do?'

'Noo*othing*,' she sobbed. 'It's not yo-ooou. It's meeee.'

She carried on sobbing for a few moments so I put my arm around her and stroked her back. 'What is it? Come on, Shazza, you can tell me.'

'Juuuu . . . ust . . . no one ever takes me seriously . . . everyone . . .' sob, sob, sob.

'What? Everyone what? Come on, you can tell me.'

Shazza wiped her eyes and sniffed. 'I'm sorry, Mac. Sorry. Just . . . well, everyone always thinks, you know, "Shazza, good for a laugh. A bit of fun and . . ."' Sob, sob. 'They don't realise that I have . . . feeeeeeeeelings . . .' And off she went, sobbing her heart out again.

Oh. My. God. I thought. What the hell do I do now?

I gently stroked her back a little longer and after a while, her sobs subsided and she turned to look at me. 'I . . . I can tell you're not like the rest of them, Mac. You're not a user . . . you're really sweet and not just here for what you can get . . .'

Oh bugger, I thought as I cuddled her in to my shoulder and realised suddenly that I was. I *was*. I was a user. The worst possible kind. And I felt *awful* about it. She laid her head on my shoulder and snuggled into my neck. I hadn't a clue what to say but it didn't matter as for her the floodgates had opened and out came pouring the whole sad story of her love life. All the boys who had come and gone in her life, dated her and snogged her and then just as she was getting keen on them, they'd dump her and move on. In between telling me all about them, she'd sob and I began to feel sorry for her as she was clearly a nice girl.

When she'd finished talking, we lay for a while in the sun and I gently stroked her hair.

'What's wrong with me?' she asked. 'Why does it always happen to me? All I want is to have a good time but no one seems to want to stay with me for long.'

'Nothing's wrong with you,' I said. 'You deserve better. You're a great girl. But . . . maybe you should play more hard to get. Boys like a challenge sometimes. Like, if they feel they have to work for something, they want it all the more.'

'Do you think?' She sniffed.

I nodded thinking, Nooooooo, actually. Sometimes you just want an easy time but I knew that no way was it going to happen here, not this afternoon. I couldn't do it to her. I couldn't take advantage of her just because I was feeling bad myself and needed distracting. I was as bad, if not worse, than all the boys she'd just listed.

I got up and fetched a beach towel from the back of the deck chair on the patio. 'Here,' I said as I covered her up. 'Cover up. Seeing you like that is doing my head in as you really are a gorgeous girl, Shazza.'

She smiled sweetly up at me. 'You're so nice, Mac.'

No, I'm not, I thought. Not nice at all. If she hadn't started crying, who knows what might have happened.

I stayed with her for another hour, made her a cup of tea

then soothed and stroked her like she was a little kid. In the end, she started smiling again but by then, I wanted to go. I didn't want to get too involved with her. And too much had happened today.

When I was ready to go, Shazza gave me a big hug.

'You've been such a sweetheart,' she said, 'and sorry I've been such a cry baby.'

'No worries,' I said. 'And you take care of yourself in future.'

'I will,' she said. 'So. Mates?'

'Definitely,' I replied.

14 Clearing the Air

'HEY THERE, MAC, NEED A LIFT?' said Mr Squires as he slowed his van down.

'Oh, yeah. Thanks,' I replied and climbed in. I'd been walking half an hour so a ride the rest of the way was great.

'So what you been up to this afternoon? Bit out of your usual way, aren't you?' he asked as we drove along.

'Oh, just visiting a friend,' I said. I didn't want to fill him in on the fact that she was a semi-naked bouncing babe type friend. He didn't need details. 'Where have you been?'

'Breakdown on the motorway. Got called out just as I was sitting down to my lunch, but business is business.'

I liked Squidge's dad and his mum. Cat told me that they were the most important people in the village when I moved down here and at first, I thought that they were like the mayor and his wife or something, but actually he's the local mechanic and she's the local hairdresser – in this place, that makes them very important. If you can't get around, you're done for and if you want to look halfway decent and not turn into a country bumpkin, you need Mrs Squires.

'Any idea of where Squidge is?' I asked. 'I've been calling him all day but he's not picked up.'

'He's taken himself off camping,' said Mr Squires. 'Up at Rame Head. I thought you were going along?'

'I was. Got distracted.'

'Ah,' he said, then smiled. 'Girl involved, by any chance?'

Several, I thought. What a day and now I have to go back and face the mad women of Anderton. I envied Squidge having parents like Mr and Mrs Squires. They seemed rock solid as a couple. Easygoing and Squidge always said that his dad was great to talk to in a crisis, because he never judged or told anyone how to behave. He just listened. Unlike my parents. Mum with her endless lists of things to do and Dad so involved in his own life and problems, I can't even approach him. I felt sad it was like that. I wished I had a dad I could turn to at times like this.

'Hey, Mr Squires,' I said as we approached the turn off to Anderton ten minutes later. 'Can I talk to you?'

'Talk to me? Sure. Shoot.'

'Girls,' I said. 'Women. Is there a secret? I sure as hell don't understand them.'

Mr Squires laughed. 'Me neither. One of life's great mysteries is the female race. So what's been going on?'

'How long have you got?'

'Long as it takes, son,' he said, smiling.

And so I told him the whole story, right from the point where Becca dumped me up until Shazza sobbing her heart out this afternoon.

Mr Squires drew up in front of our house and seemed in no hurry to get rid of me. He listened patiently then he let out a long whistle. 'Sounds like you've got yourself into a bit of a mess, lad. I remember back to when I was a teenager and it doesn't sound like it's got any easier.'

'So what do I do?'

'I reckon that the trick is to keep it clean, all the way down the line. That's my first bit of advice about women: tell the truth.'

'I've tried to. Well, sort of, anyway. It's hard with Roz as she only sees and hears what she wants to. Emily wouldn't listen at all. And Becca had already made her mind up what I was feeling before I had a chance to tell her.' I glanced up at the house. 'And then there's that lot in there. Gran, Mum and Jade. They all tell me what to do as well.'

Mr Squires laughed. 'A house full of women. You have my sympathy.'

'And they all get so emotional about everything. Some weeks it's awful in there. Talk about mood swings. Sometimes I feel like running away.'

'No need for that. You just have to learn to stand your ground. Let them know that you're in there too and you have a mind of your own.'

'That's the hard bit. I find it really difficult. I hate confrontation and I hate scenes and overreactions. Like I know they'll all be in there, waiting to hear what happened with Emily so that they can all offer advice. Sometimes I find it easiest just to button up and let them get on with it.'

'Yes, but you don't want to get walked over. It's like when I said tell the truth, sometimes you have to start with yourself. Never mind your gran or your mum or Jade or Becca or Roz or Shazza or whatever was her name?'

'Emily.'

'Emily. Thing is, what's your truth? What does Mac want?'

'I'd like to live with my dad for my A-level years. You know, go back up to London but Mum will hit the roof and anyway there's not much chance of it happening. Dad has his own female household to contend with – his new girlfriend and her daughter. And I'd like to be with Emily. No doubt about that. She's the One. Or was until I blew it.'

'OK. Start with her, then. This is my second bit of advice. Don't give up. If you really like this girl, don't give up on her. If she won't speak to you, write her a letter. And tell her the truth.'

I felt myself squirming inside. 'She's going to think I'm such a coward . . . All that stuff about asking Becca to say we were still an item . . .'

'If that's the truth, tell it. You're dead right, women are hard to understand all right but one thing I've learned is that they don't always want perfect. Sometimes when you show your more vulnerable side, they accept it. Admit you've made mistakes. Blew it. Got it all wrong. So put your cards on the table. They don't always expect us to have all the answers. Tell this Emily what you've just told me and let her decide.'

'You think?'

'Definitely. What have you got to lose?'

That's true, I thought. I've got nothing to lose. I felt better. Clearer. I was going to say how I felt. Tell it like it was. Stop trying to please everyone all the time.

'Thanks, Mr Squires,' I said as I got out of the van.

'Anytime, Mac,' he said.

As soon as I got upstairs into my room, I called Emily again. Her phone was still on voicemail and I didn't want to e-mail as it felt too impersonal for what I had to say, so I sat down at my desk and wrote her a long letter explaining everything, about Roz, about Becca and about how I felt about her.

Next I called Becca.

'Hey,' I said.

'Hey yourself,' she said.

She didn't sound too mad with me any more so I took a deep breath and continued. 'I'm sorry about before,' I said. 'You weren't to know that Emily wasn't Roz. So . . . sorry I went off at you.'

'It's OK, Mac,' she said. 'I phoned Cat to have a moan about you and she'd been speaking to Lia who knew all about Emily. So now I'm in the picture. Love of your life.' Then she giggled. 'Sorry. But it was funny in a way, wasn't it?'

She started laughing again and although I was slightly miffed at Squidge for telling Lia about Emily, I started to see the funny side too so laughed as well.

'So what happened after I'd done my Oscar performance?' she asked.

'She went off back to London. Not speaking to me.'

'Oh I am sorry, Mac. I thought you might have got it sorted with her.'

'Nope. I'm well in her bad books now.'

'Bummer. So you really like this girl, huh?'

'I do.'

'Well, if there's anything I can do to make it right again, let me know – OK?'

'Thanks. I will.'

'And if you ever need me to help out when the real Roz is around, I'm still willing.'

'Thanks, Bec, but I doubt if it will come to that. I won't be seeing her again if I can help it. In fact, I'm just about to call her and tell her that there's no chance anything is ever going to happen with us and not because I've already got a girlfriend. I'm going to tell her the truth.'

'Good for you, Mac. Telling the truth always works best in the end. But with us, mates again?'

'Mates,' I said.

Two down, one to go, I thought when I'd put the phone. Mates with Bec, mates with Shazza. Next was Roz.

'Hey, Roz,' I said when she picked up.

'Mac. How's it going?'

'Good. Listen . . . er . . . I wanted to talk to you to make a few things clear . . .'

'Oh. OK.'

'Well, what I told you about Becca. It's not strictly true.'

'Meaning?'

'It's over between us.'

'*Really?*'

'Yes. I wanted to tell you because, well this last few weeks, I've been a bit mixed up in my head but I want to be honest about everything in all my relationships from now on and . . .'

'Oh Mac, I'm *so* glad you phoned but listen . . . I've got to go now. Mum's calling me. Can we talk again tomorrow?'

'Yeah. Sure.'

Excellent, I thought after I'd put the phone down. It was going really well. And it wasn't so hard telling the truth. Mr Squires had been right. Clear the air. Tell the truth.

Next were the three witches downstairs. I'd heard them gossiping in the kitchen when I'd come in earlier and snuck upstairs before they summoned me in. But now I was just about ready for them. I threw a few things into my rucksack, took a deep breath and went downstairs.

'Oh, Mac. What happened?' asked Gran, as soon as I set foot in the kitchen. Three faces stared at me expectantly.

Tell the truth, I thought. 'I messed up,' I said. 'Roz wasn't getting the message that I didn't want to get involved so to buy myself some breathing space, I told her that I still had a girlfriend, Becca. Then I asked Becca that if she ever met Roz, to pretend that we were still an item and she thought that Emily was Roz and did a number. Emily thought I'd been lying to her about it being over with Becca and took off back to London in a huff and won't take my calls. So um . . . that brings you all up to date, I think.'

'Oh, you poor dear,' said Gran. 'What are you going to do now?'

I gave her a huge grin and hoisted my rucksack onto my shoulder. 'I know exactly what I'm going to do. I'm going camping!'

And with that, I left them all sitting at the kitchen table.

Camping

'OH WHAT A BEEEOOOOOTIFUL MOOOOOORNING,' I sang into Squidge's ear as he lay snoring in his sleeping bag. 'Come on, lazybones, it's a glorious day outside.'

Squidge opened his eyes, yawned and stretched. 'God, who invited you along?' he asked as he sat up and ran his fingers through his hair making it stick up more than normal. 'What time is it?'

'Half nine. I slept like a log.'

'Me too,' said Squidge getting out of the sleeping bag and wriggling into his jeans then he stuck his head out of the tent opening. 'How about we decamp later? Me need bacon buttie and mug of tea. How do you fancy Whitsand café?'

'Excellent choice, my blurry-eyed chum,' I replied. 'Simple pleasures.'

We'd had a brilliant night once I'd found him. I'd had a

feeling that he'd go to his favourite spot and sure enough, there he was with the tent already pitched and he was delighted that I'd come out to join him. Luckily, he'd brought plenty of supplies and we'd had a supper of baked beans and sausages cooked on a fire. Then we'd layed on our backs and watched the stars while we chatted, told jokes and generally caught up with each other. He couldn't stop laughing when I told him about Shazza.

'So much for the sympathy,' I'd said.

'I know, I know. I'm sorry but . . .' And he'd started laughing again. 'But man, just your luck. I can just see you there thinking that you're going to get some action then . . . she turns on the waterworks. Sorry, sorry but it *is* funny.'

'Becca started laughing about the mix-up with Emily. I don't know. Some friends, I have. I'm living a nightmare and you guys all think it's hilarious.'

'Well, it is,' Squidge had said. 'They should write a sitcom about you and your love life. Be hysterical.'

'Today was just *one* episode. I'm back on track now. And I'm going to take your dad's advice. I'm not going to give up with Emily.'

When we'd gone to bed in the early hours of the morning, I'd slept better than I had in weeks. My head felt calm, my purpose was clear.

* * *

After a good breakfast fry-up at the café, we went down on to the beach below for a couple of hours where Squidge took some photos then we set off back for camp. Once back there, we dismantled the tent and began to pack up.

'Blimey, it's one o'clock already,' said Squidge as he glanced at his watch. 'I said I'd meet Lia. I'll just give her a call.'

He moved off to the cliff edge and I lay back on the grass and gazed up at the sky. It had been a good time and I resolved to do it again in the near future. A female free zone, I thought – times like this should be compulsory for men everywhere.

'How about I come back to yours to brush my teeth as it's on the way?' said Squidge when he'd finished his call. 'Lia's over at Becca's so I'll go on to her house after yours.'

'Fine,' I said and we set off along the coast road and down towards the villages.

The walk back took about forty-five minutes and as we got close to Anderton, I needed to take a pee. I climbed over a fence and went behind a couple of bushes where no one could see me from the road. When I got back, Squidge had a strange look on his face.

'What?' I asked.

'Oh . . . nothing. Probably nothing. Just . . . a taxi just went past and . . . well, I think I saw someone who looked very like Roz in the back.'

'No chance. What would she be doing down here? Must have been someone who looks like her.'

It couldn't be her, I told myself as a sinking feeling hit the pit of my stomach. She wouldn't? Would she?

'M*aac*! Surprise,' said Roz as she burst out of the front door when we reached home. She rushed forward and gave me an enormous bear hug.

Behind her, I could see Squidge creasing up laughing, then he gave me the thumbs up. When she let me go, he walked close: 'The Mac sitcom part two. I watch with respect and anticipation.'

'Do not leave,' I whispered. *'Please.'*

Mum was watching from the porch with an amused expression on her face and behind her was Gran who looked like she was having a hard time not laughing as well. Oh, sell tickets, why don't you? I thought. Invite the whole village.

'Good, Mac, there you are,' said Mum. 'I was just about to drive Roz up to find you. Isn't this a lovely surprise?'

I nodded with a clenched jaw. 'Just lovely,' I said through gritted teeth.

'Come on, everyone,' said Mum. 'I'll put the kettle on and make us a nice cup of tea and Roz, you can tell me how your mum and dad are and all about London.'

'Er, just a sec, Mum. Er . . . can I have a private moment with Roz first?'

Roz smiled coyly and slipped her hand into mine. Behind her, I thought Squidge was going to lose it altogether as he began to have a coughing fit.

'Soooomething cough . . . cough . . . caught in my throat. Neeeeed glass of water,' he spluttered and just about fell into the house.

I will kill him later, I thought as I watched him go in. Roz had her back to the open front door and through it I could see Squidge leaning against the wall, laughing, and worst of all, Gran was joining in.

'Roz,' I said as firmly as I could. 'What on earth are you doing here?'

Roz put her arms round my neck. 'It was after what you said on the phone yesterday,' she said as she nuzzled into my neck.

'What? What did I say?'

'About it being over between you and Becca.'

'Yes,' I said as I took her arms, put them back down by her side and stepped away. 'It is over between us but why would that make you come down here?'

She stepped close to me. 'Oh, come on, Mac. I know why you told me that. You said you'd been mixed up but now you were clear . . .'

I was missing something, I thought as she nuzzled in again. I glanced up at the house. By now, Squidge and Gran were at the window staring out. Squidge did a kissy kissy face.

'OK, Roz. I'll tell you why I told you that . . .'

'You don't have to do that. I *know*,' said Roz. 'You're so sweet, so shy . . .'

I gently pushed her off me again.

'Maaac. Why are you being like this?' she asked as she turned and caught Gran and Squidge who were still staring out the window. 'Oh. It's because we're being watched.'

She grabbed my hand and began to lead me round to the back of the house. I had to do something fast.

'No, Roz. You've got the wrong . . .'

As usual, Roz wasn't listening and she leaned into me and began to snog me.

'N . . . no . . .' I said trying to wriggle away from her. 'Roz . . . really . . . we have to talk . . .'

She put her hand up to my lips. 'No, Mac. This isn't the time for words . . .' she said as she leaned in to kiss me again.

'OH YES IT IS,' said a stern voice behind us.

I turned to see my audience had grown. Becca, Cat and Lia were standing in the rose alcove. It was Becca who had spoken. She stepped forward and stood in front of Roz.

'And you're Roz, I presume?'

'Yes,' said Roz, squaring up to her.

'Just checking,' said Becca and gave me a conspiratorial look. She came and stood by me and took my hand. 'Well, Roz, Mac is *my* boyfriend and I'd like to know what you think you were just doing?'

Roz flushed red. 'And you are?'

I began to feel ill. 'Oh sorry, er . . . introductions. Yes . . . Roz, this is Becca. And over there is Cat and you know Lia . . .' I glanced at the side of the house and as expected, Squidge and Gran had moved to a window where they had a good view of the back garden. 'And over there, as you know, are Squidge and my gran who no doubt will be joined by Mum and Jade at any moment.'

'Oh. So *you're* Becca,' said Roz and put her hand in my other one. 'Yes, Mac has told me *all* about you so you can let go of his hand. He told me that it's over between you.'

Becca held onto my hand even tighter. 'Oh he did, did he?'

'Yes, yesterday.'

'Ah,' said Becca. 'Well, we got back together last night. Didn't we, Mac? So *I'm* Mac's girlfriend.'

'No,' said a small voice from the alcove. We all turned. It was Cat who had spoken this time and she looked close to bursting out laughing. 'No. *I'm* Mac's girlfriend. After seeing you last night Becca, he came over to see *me*. Sorry, but it's true. *I'm* Mac's girlfriend.'

'No,' said Lia in a shocked voice. 'After seeing you, Cat,

he came to see me. *I'm* Mac's girlfriend now. Go on – tell her, Mac. Tell her.'

Lia, Cat and Becca couldn't keep it up any longer and creased up laughing.

Roz turned to look at me. She looked pale. 'What the hell is going on, Mac? Tell them. *Tell* them.'

I looked at all the faces around me and wanted the ground to open up and swallow me. This was insane. Really insane. In the recesses of my mind, I heard Mr Squires's voice. Tell the truth. Tell the truth.

'None of them is my girlfriend,' I said. 'None of them.'

Some of the colour reappeared on Roz's face along with a look of smugness.

'I knew it,' she said as she turned to Becca. 'And I don't know what kind of joke you think this is but I can assure you that it's not funny. Look. I know it must be hard to hear but Mac and I have something really special and we go back a long way. Years, in fact. He called me yesterday to . . .'

'Tell her, Mac,' said Becca quietly.

Tell the truth, said the voice in my head. I didn't want to humiliate Roz in front of everyone so I pulled her away further down into the garden. 'Give us a moment,' I said to Lia, Cat and Becca who had now stopped acting like some kind of mental Greek chorus. They turned and went into the house to join the rest of the audience.

'Look, Roz, sorry about that,' I said when we were alone.

She stuck out her bottom lip. 'You should be . . . But I don't blame her for trying. I mean, I wouldn't give you up without a fight. I feel sorry for her. But I'm not going to let her ruin what we have.'

'No,' I said. '*No, Roz.*'

She looked puzzled. 'What do you mean, "no"?'

'I mean, no. We don't have anything. At least not on my part. That's what I was trying to tell you yesterday but you had to go before I got to it. Yes, it's over between Becca and me but it was over before I even came up to London. I used her as an excuse to put you off. Only it didn't. That's what I was trying to tell you yesterday. It's not going to happen with us, Roz. You're great girl. You'll meet someone else. Can we just be friends?'

'Blah blah blah blah blah,' said Roz as she pursed her lips and folded her arms in front of her.

I felt rotten. This is just what I hate, I thought as her eyes welled up with tears. I hate it when girls get upset.

'I'm sorry,' I said and tried to put my arm round her.

She shrugged me off. 'You will be,' she said. 'And you can forget the cartooning gig with my dad. I'm going to tell him that you used me to get to him. Your cartoons weren't any good anyway. Too safe and bland. Scared to say what you really feel, just like you. And you've blown your double dare

153

so that's a trillion years bad luck. Now phone me a taxi, I'm not staying here in this horrible place another minute.'

Exit a very pissed-off Roz, twenty minutes later.

She wasn't the only one who'd had enough. As soon as she'd gone, I went up to my room, locked the door and threw myself onto the bed. I felt like kicking something or someone. I punched a few cushions, got up and kicked my desk, almost broke my toe, then threw myself back down onto the bed again. First Emily, then the episode with Shazza and now Roz. No wonder everyone thought it was so funny. Everyone except for me that is. I didn't think it was funny at all. Now Emily and Roz both hated me. I hadn't even gone back to London but already I was going to have the reputation from hell and God knows what the taxi driver who picked them both up must think.

I checked my phone to see if by any miracle there was a message from Emily. But nothing – I should have known. Plus she wouldn't have got my letter yet. Just four texts: one from Squidge, one from Becca, one from Lia and one from Cat, all saying sorry and to come over to where they were. Squidge had taken them off to Becca's house just before Roz had left as he could tell just by looking at me that I was in a state. I didn't feel like talking to them. Not for a long while.

I got up, found my pad and pencils and sat down at my desk. 'So you think my cartoons are safe and bland, do you Roz? You and your stupid double dare. That trillion years bad luck started the day you first called me. Well, I'll show you . . .'

In a fit of rage I began to draw.

First Roz. I drew her as a mean looking spider in the middle of a vast web caught in which was a fly that looked very like me.

Next was Emily. I drew her as a tiny frightened bird locked in a cage at a desk with a typewriter and reams of paper flying everywhere like feathers.

The floodgates had opened and I was away. I pulled out the photos of Alistair, Otis and Amanda and studied them closely.

Who cares? I thought as I began to caricature them. No one's going to see these now, so what does it matter how they turn out.

I worked until the early hours of the morning. Most of the drawings ended up in the bin but I carried on as I knew I wouldn't be able to sleep until I got everything out of my system. By two thirty, I felt wasted. I'd done it. Four caricatures of the four new faces were beginning to take shape. Four caricatures that no one would ever get to see.

16   Love Hurts

DAD TURNED UP the following week. On Wednesday, to be precise. I was in the art room after school when Jade phoned to let me know that he'd arrived. I'd been working on the cartoons I'd started on Sunday night as even though I knew I couldn't send them in, I could still use them for my portfolio. I'd had a breakthrough on the one for Alistair and drawn and redrawn it. Seeing as he's an actor, I'd depicted him as a Hamlet-type character with a puffed out chest and skinny legs in a pair of tights and a very big handsome head grinning widely with gleaming Hollywood style teeth. He looked as cocky and debonair as he was in life. I knew he'd hate it but it was better than my previous bland attempts which flattered him. The ones for Otis and Amanda didn't look half bad either. Otis on a stage with a huge shadow looming behind him, his features exaggerated to make him look like a sinister insect. And Amanda, I'd drawn as an angel dressed in a choir outfit in a church stained glass window. She looked exuberant, her face turned up, arms raised, singing her heart out and cracking all the glass in the window.

As soon as I'd taken the call from Jade, I packed up fast and set off for home. On my way back, I felt angry with Dad. Why had he come midweek when he knew Jade and I were at school? The whole purpose of asking him down was so that we could spend some time with him but there was no way I could bunk off school.

Jade was sitting out on the front porch when I got home. She was all hunched over, staring out at the bay and didn't notice when I approached.

'Where is he?' I asked.

She jerked her thumb back towards inside the house. 'Talking to Mum in the kitchen. He wanted a few minutes with her, then he wants to talk to us.'

'And where's Gran?'

'Made herself scarce when Dad arrived. Said she might have to punch him if she'd stayed.'

'What are they talking about?'

Jade shrugged.

The front door was open so I tiptoed inside and stood in

the alcove. I could hear voices coming from the kitchen so I crept a bit closer and listened.

'Do you want to tell them or should I?' asked Dad.

There was a pause before Mum spoke. 'Neil,' she said in a cold, even voice, 'this is *entirely* between you and Jade and Mac. You've got a cheek even suggesting that I tell them. Don't be such a coward . . . but then you always were, weren't you? Any bad news and you always left it up to me.'

'I wouldn't call it bad news,' said Dad. 'And I'm sorry you feel that way and I'm sorry . . .'

'OK, sorry too, wrong word. Not bad news, difficult news. They've had a lot of readjustments to make, a *lot*, and now you're asking them to take this on board as well. It's typical you would ask me to do it but you made your bed, you have to lie in it.'

Whatever they were talking about, it didn't seem to be going well, I thought as any fantasy I had about them getting back together flew out the window fast. I had a good idea of what Dad wanted to say to Jade and I. And it wasn't that he wanted to get back with Mum.

'I know, I know,' said Dad. 'I'll do it. And . . . I'd like to say that I think you've done a fantastic job with them. You've provided much more of a stable influence than I ever could have, although things are picking up . . .'

'Well, they're good kids, both of them, but really, Neil,

you have to do this yourself. Honestly, it's so typical of you to try and worm your way out of it. That was half of the trouble with us. You would never take any responsibility . . .'

'Please, Sarah. Don't start. I didn't come down here to argue and rake over old ground.'

I didn't want to hear any more. I coughed so that they'd realise that I was there.

'Mac? Is that you?' asked Mum.

'Yeah,' I said as I stepped forward. 'Hi, Dad.'

'Mac! Hi,' said Dad.

'So what is it you wanted to say to us?' I asked.

Dad glanced over at Mum. She got up and went to the door as I put my portfolio down and sat at the table.

'I'll go and fetch Jade,' said Mum and went out into the hall.

Dad and I sat in an awkward silence as we waited for Jade. I knew exactly what he was going to say but I wasn't going to do it for him.

'Can I see your work?' asked Dad, pointing at my portfolio.

'Nothing to see, really.'

'Oh, come on. I'd love to see what you've been up to,' said Dad getting up and putting my portfolio on the table. Part of me longed to show him all my work and see what he thought as a fellow artist. Another part of me didn't want to get all matey over it like we used to as our art was the one common area we had that was guaranteed to get us talking. He flicked through and I could tell by his face that he liked what he saw. He laughed out loud at the one of the three witches of Anderton but I kept my face straight. I wasn't going to make it easy for him? He hadn't bothered to try and see my work for almost a year so why should I get all enthusiastic with him? When he got to the latest drawings of the new faces, he stopped.

'These the ones for the magazine?'

'Were. I'm not doing it any more.'

Dad flicked through and let out a low whistle. 'These are good, Mac. I mean *really* good. These are the best you've done so far. Why do you say you're not doing it any more?'

'Fell out with Roz.'

Dad smiled. 'Ah. Hence the spider drawing. I thought I recognised her.'

I nodded.

'What are you going to do with them?'

'Portfolio. For college.'

'But why not show them to Roz's dad? You fell out with her not him.'

'She got me the gig. She said I can forget it. We're not even speaking now.'

'I see. Right. Er . . . mind if I take them? All your latest stuff. I'd like to have some of your work up at the flat. To remind me of you.'

'Not quite finished some of them.'

'Tell you what, then. How about I take them, photocopy them then I'll send them straight back to you?'

'Whatever,' I said. I knew I could have got photocopies done for him at school but I didn't really care what happened to them any more.

Jade came through a few moments later and sat sullenly at the table. I got a feeling that she knew what Dad was going to say as well.

'How long are you down for?' I finally asked.

'Just for this evening,' said Dad. 'I'm driving back tonight. You know how it is, got a job on for tomorrow.'

'But Dad,' I said, 'why can't you stay longer? You haven't been down since we moved here. And why didn't you come at a weekend when we could spend some proper time together?'

'Yeah,' said Jade. 'We are your real family and I haven't seen you for ages. At least Mac saw you when he was up in London.'

'Only for a few hours,' I said and I knew my tone was bitter. 'I was told I couldn't stay there, remember? Tamara's sleepover that didn't happen?'

Dad looked like he'd rather be anywhere else than in our kitchen in Cornwall and I knew that maybe I sounded like a sulky kid but I couldn't help it. Part of me felt angry with him and I think Jade felt the same way. OK, so he'd had an affair and messed everything up with Mum but that wasn't our fault.

'Listen, kids . . .' he started.

'I'm not a kid,' said Jade. 'I'm fifteen, in case you hadn't noticed.'

'OK, sorry. But please, listen. I do have some news. Well sort of. I wanted to talk it over with you first because despite what you think, I do respect your feelings and I'm sorry for all the . . . all the upset I've caused.'

Jade and I glanced over at each other. Although we have many differences in our day to day life and often act like we hate each other, we both knew that we were in this together.

'So, what is it you're here to say?' I asked. I wanted him to get it over with.

'Sonia,' he said. 'As you know Mac, we had a bit of an . . .'

'Argument,' I said. 'She wanted more of a commitment from you.'

Dad nodded. 'And . . . I've given it a lot of thought and I'd like to. Make more of a commitment, that is.'

'You mean marry her,' I said.

Dad nodded again. 'But first I wanted to tell you.'

'Tell us or *ask* us?' asked Jade.

'Where's Sonia now?' I asked.

'Back at the flat.'

'Then you've already asked her, haven't you?'

I knew she wouldn't have gone back if he hadn't offered her what she wanted. The whole reason she'd walked out on him was because he wouldn't give her commitment. There would have been no reason for her to go back if he hadn't.

'Well, sort of . . . yes. I have put it to her.'

'So why are you asking us, then? What's the point? We don't even figure in the equation, just like we didn't before when you went ahead and had the affair that blew everything out of the water. Don't remember anyone asking us then what we felt and would we mind moving house and changing school.'

I couldn't help it. Over a year's feelings of resentment and anger were threatening to come pouring out.

Dad sighed and looked at the floor. I glanced over at him and he looked close to tears. I felt my throat constrict and knew I was in danger of crying myself. God, this sucks, I thought.

'Anyone want a cup of tea?' I asked getting up and going over to the kettle. I didn't want to break down in front of him and Jade and I *really* didn't want to see him cry.

'Yes, please,' said Dad seeming glad of the distraction. 'Yes, cup of tea.'

'When?' asked Jade.

'Er, now,' said Dad and attempted a smile.

Jade rolled her eyes. 'The wedding, not the tea.'

'Right. Um. Not got any dates as yet. Nothing definite. Look. I know it may not appear like this to you but I really do care what you two think. If you're dead against it, I'll put a stop to it right now. You are my kids, I mean . . . yeah, you are my *kids,* no disrespect meant to your ages. You'll always be first in my book and I need to know that you're OK about things before I go ahead and book anything like dates or venues.'

Jade sat back in her chair and looked at Dad through narrowed eyes. 'Do you love Sonia?' she asked.

'Very much,' said Dad quietly.

'More than Mum?' I asked.

Dad shifted uncomfortably in his chair. 'It's different . . .'

Jade sat back up straight and looked over at me. 'Well, I can tell you now that I have no objection. Sonia's OK. As long as she doesn't try and act like she's our mother or anything naff like that. And Tamara, well she's a kid but I like her too. But, Dad . . . if you say that we come first then . . . I'd like to see more of you. It's like you've disappeared this last year.'

'I know,' said Dad, 'but things were . . . well . . . difficult between your mother and me. I didn't want to rock the boat more than was necessary. I wanted to give you time to settle.'

And avoid any nasty scenes, I thought, as I poured boiling water into three cups. Dad's a coward, I thought. Mum was right. And I've been in danger of being just like him. He's where I've got it all from. Trying to please, say what people want to hear, as he said, anything not to upset the boat. But it doesn't work. The boat gets upset anyhow and it's better to be straight in the beginning. At least that way, everyone knows where they are and what they're dealing with.

'Mac?' asked Dad.

I still had my back to him and didn't turn around. 'I'm not going to stand in your way,' I said. 'You do what you want. You probably will, anyway.'

I knew it wasn't the response he was probably hoping for but I wasn't going to burst into song and congratulate him either. He was the one coming out of the whole situation with what he wanted. A new wife, someone to be with whereas Mum was on her own. And we were still hundreds of miles away from London and our old life.

After he'd gone, the atmosphere in the house was quiet. It was like everyone needed time alone to digest things.

Mum took a glass of wine to the picnic table at the

bottom of the garden and sat staring into the bushes. She looked not unlike how Jade had at the front when I first arrived home. Poor Mum, I thought as I watched her out of the kitchen window and wondered what was going on in her head.

She was wearing make-up for the first time in months and I noticed she'd made an effort with her hair for once. It was loose on her shoulders whereas most days now, she wore it pulled back in a clip like she couldn't be bothered. Back in London, she used to have her hair done every week at the hairdresser's and it always looked glossy and chic.

I got the wine out of the fridge and took it down to her.

'Would madam care for another glass of wine?'

She looked up and smiled. 'Actually, I would.'

I filled her glass and sat opposite her. 'You OK?'

She nodded slowly. 'You?'

'Yeah. Er . . . guess you heard the news then?'

'Yep.'

I sat and looked out over the garden with her for a while. I really wanted to say something but wasn't sure what.

'You look really nice today.'

Mum touched her hair. 'Thanks. Thought I'd better make a bit of an effort.'

'Well you look good and I'm sorry it didn't work out.'

'Thanks, Mac. Oh but . . . *oh*! You didn't think that I'd done myself up because I wanted him back?'

'Er . . . I . . . I did wonder.'

She leaned over and put a hand over one of mine. 'No, Mac. I just didn't want him to think I'd turned into an old bag who'd let herself go.'

'No chance of that. So you're OK about him getting remarried?'

Mum considered my question for a few moments then she nodded. 'Yeah. Yeah. I'm OK with it. Well, as OK as I ever will be. He's moved on. I knew that. And it's not exactly like I didn't expect it. Good luck to him.'

'I guess . . . but you didn't ask for any of this.'

'No. No I didn't but . . . OK. Mac, let me tell you something. I guess I should have told you a long time ago but . . . things weren't right between your dad and me for a long time before he had the affair. And although yes, I wish in some ways it hadn't happened like that, it was on the cards. We were drifting apart. I had my work. He had . . . well, his life, his plans. I think we wanted to make it work long after it was clear that things were wrong, because of you and Jade.'

'But why wasn't it working?'

Mum sighed. 'Oh . . . many reasons. We're like chalk and cheese. I'm a doer, he's a dreamer. I'm a talker, as you know, no trouble saying what I think. He could never express his feelings at all. It used to drive me mad. And all his plans that never came to anything. In the meantime, there were bills to be paid. I mean, I will always have fond feelings for your father, we were together too long not to, but he's a . . . a Peter Pan. Never grew up. Living in Never-Neverland. Always a new scheme in his head, always with another dream to follow that never came to anything. I reckon it's OK if you have no responsibilities and it used to be in the beginning when we were both young but everything changed when you and Jade came along. One of us had to grow up and in our case, it was me.'

'Mum, can I ask you something?'

'Sure.'

'When you and Dad split up and the house in Islington was sold, why didn't you buy another place up there. Smaller. We could have coped. Your catering work was going so well and I'm sure you must miss it and London life. So why didn't you use money from the sale of the house to buy another one?'

'Big house, big mortgage,' said Mum. 'There wasn't actually a lot left once we'd paid the mortgage off and what there was I wanted to put away for you and Jade for when you go to college. Simple as that. If there had been enough money, believe me, we'd have stayed up there.'

As we sat together, Mum sipping her wine, for the first time I began to really think about what she had done for us.

It was always her that had been up late at night doing the bills and the accounts. It was always her who organised anything in the house. Got us to school on time. Picked us up. Ferried us about. Dad may be an absent father now but when I thought back, he was then too. It was always Mum who'd been around.

As the light began to fade, I got up to go back inside.

'Sure you're OK, Mum?'

She nodded. 'Just thinking how everything changes, hey?'

'Sure does,' I replied and set off up the garden then I turned back. 'Mum . . . er . . . I . . . just . . . thanks for . . . I don't know, for being there. Then and now.'

Mum smiled. 'Anytime Mac. You're my boy.'

I went back into the house and up to my room. I glanced out of my window at the garden and she was still sitting there. A solitary figure silhouetted in the dusk. Love hurts, I thought, no matter what age you are.

17 Second Chance

THE MELLOW MOOD that was around after Dad's visit didn't last long. Mum was soon back into her bionic routine ordering everyone around and Jade went back to being her usual sarky self.

True to Dad's word, he sent my cartoons back to me with a note saying that he looked forward to seeing Jade and me at half-term and that Sonia and Tamara were pushing off for a few days so that we'd have plenty of room to stay. It was something to look forward to – I'd been feeling badly about my behaviour to him when he was here and wanted a chance to make things better between us. After talking to Mum, I understood that it wasn't just the affair that broke them up. I couldn't begrudge him his second chance even though it meant that Tamara got the spare room so any chance of me going up there to live was a non-starter.

The day that my cartoons came back in the post, I opened them and dashed off to school, leaving them on the dresser in the kitchen. When I got home that night Mum had obviously been looking at them. So had Gran. In fact she'd Blu-tacked the one I'd done of her, Mum and Jade as the witches onto the fridge.

'Oh, God!' I gasped when I saw it there. 'I . . . I didn't mean for you to see that . . .'

Gran laughed. 'Why ever not? It's great. I love it. I'm going to have it framed and put in the dining room.'

'No Gran . . . Jade will kill me.'

'She should be flattered that such a talented artist chooses her as a subject.'

'No . . . *Please* put it away.'

'OK. For now. But I'm going to ask her permission when she gets back.'

Just what I need, I thought. Another girl on the list of those who hate me. And we'd been getting on marginally better since Dad's visit as well.

Mum hadn't said anything. But I knew she would sooner or later.

'Er . . . sorry, Mum,' I said and attempted a sheepish grin as soon as Gran had left the room. 'I don't really think you're an old witch.'

To my surprise, she smiled.

'I guess I am sometimes,' she said. 'But how come you never showed me these drawings before?'

'No point showing them to anyone after what's happened.'

'What do you mean?'

'When Roz stormed off that day, she told me to forget the cartooning job. Don't forget it's her dad who's editor. And she got me in.'

Mum rolled her eyes. 'And you're going to let that stop you?'

'Duh. Yeah. Don't think I fancy another encounter with her if I can help it and I don't think that she'll be in a hurry to see or speak to me again.'

It was over a week since the Sunday she'd stormed off and I hadn't heard a peep out of her although I had texted her to say sorry because in the days after she'd gone, I began to feel rotten about what had happened when she was down here. OK so I didn't want her to be my girlfriend but I didn't want our strange friendship to end like that either.

Mum sifted through my drawings and sighed.

'What?' I asked.

'Sometimes you're just like your father.'

'Well I *am* his son,' I said. 'I'm bound to have some of his characteristics.'

'No need to be sarcastic, Mac. No, what I mean is using an excuse not to send your work off.'

'It's not an excuse.'

'Yes, it is. Your dad was the same and I knew what was behind it. Fear. Fear of rejection. He couldn't stand anyone to say anything bad about his work so he'd deliberate about sending it off, making up excuses. That was his trouble. He did some brilliant work but no one ever got to see it.'

'This is different. Roz told me to forget the whole deal. Plus those drawings aren't exactly flattering, particularly the one of Alistair. They'll hate them. Sometimes you have to play the game when trying to get ahead. You have to be liked.'

Mum looked through them again. 'So you'd have sent off the other ones you did. I saw them. The ones that were more flattering but not as good as these?'

'Yes. No. Oh, I don't know. What's the point of even having this conversation?'

'Because I think these drawings are great, Mac. Really good. And you know as well as I that in everything creative, it has to come from the heart, not from fear. Fear of whether people like you or not. If you act like a people-pleaser, everything you do will come across as mediocre. You have to express your true feelings and that comes across in these.' She smiled. 'Especially in the witchy one. See, it's not exactly kind to me but I can recognise that it's a good drawing and I know you don't feel like that all the time. Don't be afraid to express what's in you, Mac. Good and bad, light and dark.'

'OK. OK. Then I'll tell you what I feel. You might say I'm acting like Dad used to. Well you're acting towards me like you used to with him. Telling me what to do just like you used to tell him. Taking over. It's you who's got the problem, not me. Always trying to control people and tell them how to live their life.'

For a moment I thought Mum was going to blow her top but she took a deep breath.

'Sorry, Mac . . . you're right. I know I can get carried away sometimes but it's only because I want the best for you. But you're right . . . you have to make your own decisions.'

'Thank you,' I said and picked up my drawings. 'And my decision is that these stay where they are. In my portfolio.'

As I got up to put the drawings back in their envelope, I noticed some writing on the back of Dad's note that I hadn't seen earlier.

P.S.: Just to let you know, Peter Morrisey was round last night. Remember him? He's Head of Foundation now at Chelsea Arts. He saw your drawings and was very impressed. Said that if your other work is up to that standard, he'd like to see you when the time comes and you're applying to colleges. So keep him in mind. His college is one of the best and he thinks you've got a great future in front of you. So maybe something came out of

*going for the cartooning job after all. Not what you
expected but in life, when does it ever turn out that way?*

   Love

   Dad

   *P.P.S.: I still think you should send your caricatures off.
What have you got to lose?*

I thought back to what Mum had said about me being like
Dad and how he'd done some brilliant stuff but been afraid of
rejection. I knew that it was partly true in my case. I didn't
want anyone looking at my work and declaring it crap. But
Mum was right and so was Dad. What did I have to lose? In
art, you couldn't please all the people all the time. I knew
that. There were bound to be people who didn't like my style.
I shouldn't let it stop me. And I did feel more confident after
reading what Dad said about Peter Morrisey's comments.

   Maybe I was in with a chance. It was worth finding out
at least. So what that Roz said to forget sending off my
drawings, I thought. She doesn't control me and she doesn't
control her dad's decisions for the magazine. I picked out
my caricatures. I'd photocopy them tomorrow (I
remembered what Mr Williams had said about not sending
in originals) and I'd send them off.

   Mr Williams could only say no. If I got rejected, so be it.
No one could say I hadn't tried.

18

Déja Vu

AT HALF-TERM, Jade and I got the train up to London and went to stay with Dad for a few days as arranged. Although I had to spend some of the time studying for my GCSEs, we still had a totally brilliant break and Dad made a real effort. He took us to the movies, bowling, out for lunch and I was able to tell him that I was OK about him remarrying. He seemed genuinely relieved and promised that in the future, he would make more of an effort to be involved in our lives.

One evening over pizza in a local café, he asked if I still wanted to live up in London.

I shrugged. 'Not thinking about it any more. I know it's not on the cards.'

'Well, don't write the idea off completely,' he said. 'Sonia and I have been talking and when we get married, we want to make a fresh start altogether. There's not much space in my flat and both of us feel that we'd like to find a new place. A place that's neither mine, nor hers but ours. So . . . we're going to look around. Ideally I'd like to find somewhere with more bedrooms. One for you and Jade so that you can come and go as you please and think of it as a second home. Nothing definite, as we haven't started looking yet and we don't quite know what we can afford yet, but that's what I'd like.'

'Thanks, Dad,' I said. For a moment, I felt my hopes rise but then I asked myself, is this just another of Dad's dreams? It could well be. I knew he didn't earn a fortune as a freelancer and Sonia was an actress. It was feast or famine for her too as jobs came in or didn't. However, I appreciated the gesture. It meant a lot even it was one of Dad's pie-in-the-sky fantasies. And if it came to fruition, it would be brilliant to know that I had a room when I wanted to visit London.

In between times with Dad, I was able to go over to Islington and hang out with my old mates, Max and Andy It was great to see them again and catch up and both of them urged me to apply to the sixth-form colleges that they'd applied to. The idea was beginning to have less and less appeal, though. Something had changed in me since the day that Dad came down to Cornwall. Until then, all I'd been thinking about was myself and I'd blamed Mum for uprooting us. Now I could see what she'd sacrificed for us and I didn't want to abandon her. Especially now that Dad was getting remarried. I didn't want her to feel that everyone was deserting her to move on with their lives leaving her unable to go anywhere. There would be a time to leave home later, when I went to uni.

I checked my mobile every day in the hope that Emily might have called. She'd have got my letter ages ago and I'd even e-mailed her a message that I'd be up in London but there was no reply and I knew better than to keep on at her like a sad stalker.

I also checked it in the hope that there might be a message from the magazine but all was quiet on that front too.

At least I was still sleeping well at night. There was nothing more I could have done on either score.

On our last day, Jade had gone off to Camden Lock with some of her old school friends and Andy and Max were busy, so I mooched around the flat.

'Want to do something?' asked Dad.

'What?'

'Movie?'

'What's on?'

'I'll go and look,' said Dad.

As he was looking through the local paper, my phone rang. I picked up and walked into the kitchen.

'Mac?'

'Emily?'

'Are you still in London?'

'Yeah. Leaving on the four o'clock train this afternoon.'

'Where are you?'

'Highgate. Where are you?'

'Crouch End. Fancy coming over?'

Do I fancy coming over? I thought after I'd put the phone down. Understatement of the year.

'Good news?' asked Dad as I went back into join him.

'Could be.' I grinned. 'Can we do a movie next time? It looks like my luck may be about to change.'

Emily lived in a ground-floor flat on one of the streets off the Broadway. It had an old fashioned feel to it and was just the kind of place I'd imagined her living in, walls lined with bookshelves groaning with the weight of hundreds of books. Old rugs scattered about. Battered comfy looking furniture.

'Where's your mum?' I asked after she'd let me in and shown me around.

'Oh, some conference or other. She won't be back until late tonight.'

Yabadabadoo, another chance, I thought, as she indicated for me to sit down then sat at the other end of the sofa herself.

'I . . . I got your letter,' she said. 'And I just got your messages and I'm sorry I didn't get back to you earlier. I couldn't face spending half-term here with time on my hands to go over the whole Michael thing again, so I got the train up to Edinburgh to see Dad. I've been up there and only got back this morning and found the messages that you were in London. I called you straight away as I was afraid that I might have missed you. And to tell the truth, I'd been thinking of phoning you, anyway. I . . . I guess I was a bit hasty. Acted like a real drama queen rushing off like that. I should have known that there was more to the story. So, sorry. Guess my head was a little messed up then.' She laughed. 'And by the sound of your letter so was yours. You didn't half complicate things for yourself by asking Becca to act like your girlfriend to put Roz off. Why didn't you just tell her the truth? That you didn't fancy her?'

'Because I am . . . *was* an almighty coward. I've told her since though. Came clean. She didn't like it one bit.'

'Unrequited love. It's a bummer.'

'Is that how you feel? About Michael?'

'A bit. Still, you can't make people be with you if they don't want to can you? I'm OK about it now. Accepted it was not meant to be.'

'Really?'

She smiled. 'Yeah, really. I feel like I've let go at last. And it's OK, I feel good. Free. It did me good to get away up to Scotland. It cleared my head and I got started on a new book up there. And now I feel like I'm coming back to a new chapter.'

'Apt example for a writer.' I grinned. She did seem different. Not as fragile and more sure of what she wanted. We sat and chatted for ages about relationships and how complicated they could be and I told her all about Dad's visit to Cornwall and how he was getting remarried. As we talked, she leaned back on the sofa and put her feet on my lap so I massaged her toes.

At last, I thought, we can start back where we left off when Becca butted in.

After I'd finished massaging her feet, she moved over to me on the sofa and leaned her head against my chest. All the feelings I'd felt before came flooding back and my insides turned to liquid.

She turned her face up to meet mine and once again I looked into her eyes.

'Dêja vu,' I smiled down at her.

'Dêja vu,' she smiled back.

Just as our lips were about to touch, the phone rang. She jumped slightly.

'Do you want to get it?' I asked.

She shook her head and leaned back into me. 'Answering machine's on. It's probably Mum checking in.'

There was a beep from the machine and a boy's voice.

'Emily. Emily. Are you there?'

Emily stiffened.

'It's me. Michael. Listen. I know you're back today as I've been calling all week and your mum told me. Look . . . I made the most ginormous mistake. I've been such a fool . . . Please if you're there, pick up. I've been going insane thinking that I might have lost you . . .'

Emily sat up.

I listened.

Emily listened.

'Please, please Emily if you're there. Pick up . . .'

Emily looked at me apologetically then got up to take the call.

I knew I was history.

I didn't wait until she'd finished her call. I could tell by her voice that she was choked to hear from him. I crept out into the hall, let myself out of the flat and made my way back to Dad's so that he could take me to the station to meet Jade.

Going Public

19

'SO MUCH FOR MY great experience with women,' I said to Squidge as we sat down at Cawsand Bay after school on the Monday after half-term. The sun was shining, the beach was busy with early holidaymakers and Squidge and I had decided to take a break from revision and had taken our easels down there to do some work. We'd decided to do some watercolours to go in our portfolios because when the time came for interviews for college, the tutors would want to see work in a variety of mediums. As we painted, I told Squidge all about my weekend and afternoon with Emily.

'Go on, laugh. I know you want to. Episode three in the Mac sitcom.'

Squidge shook his head. 'No. I'm not going to laugh this time. I know how much you liked Emily.

'Yeah I did. She's special. Not someone to have a quick

fling with and I did want to, you know, play the field a bit before I got into anything serious. Date a few girls. Remember that was the reason I wanted to break up with Becca in the first place?'

'I do remember. So that you could sample the whole fruit bowl etc. etc. and not just one.'

I laughed. 'Yeah. Suppose every fruit bowl has a mixture of fruit. Melons, bananas, mangoes plus a few lemons.'

'Who was the melon? Oh, of course,' Squidge put his hands to his chest and indicated large boobs. 'Shazza. Big melons! Who was the lemon?'

'Need you ask?'

'Have you heard from Roz?'

I shook my head. 'Nope. I texted her a few times to say sorry about what happened down here but I guess she's still sore.'

'Or sour if she's a lemon,' Squidge said with a grin.

'She wasn't that bad. Not really. I can't say I blame her for how she reacted. It wasn't all her fault. I could have been more straight with her in the beginning.'

'And it has all been experience,' said Squidge. 'Maybe not the kind you were thinking about, but it has been *experience*.'

'Tell me about it. My mission to understand women is still ongoing. So far, the only two things I've learned is that it's important to say what you feel and the second is that girls are an alien species. They seem to make up their own rules then break them the next day. In fact, I may take a breather from them for a while. They do my head in.'

'Yeah right,' said Squidge. 'That is until the next time. Still, the one good thing is that you did those cartoons. You'll always have those to show for it all.'

'Even if they didn't make the magazine.'

'Yeah. Still no word?'

'Nope. I thought at least they'd have sent a note saying thanks but no thanks or sent them back. I did send the required stamped addressed envelope. Good job I sent copies and not the originals as they're probably in a bin somewhere.'

'At least you did it.'

'Yep. All because of a stupid double dare. But at least I won't get a trillion years' bad luck as I fulfilled both the requirements. I went up to London, stayed with Roz and I did the cartoons for the magazine. So my luck ought to be changing.'

'Any minute now,' said Squidge as he nudged me and I looked up to see that two pretty blonde girls in bikinis were coming over to look at our paintings.

And they were the first of many. As we sat painting, just about every girl that went past, stopped to comment or flirt (plus some boys too but they mainly stopped to throw some insult our way). They didn't bother me as, without realising it, we'd lucked into a ready-made opener for meeting girls. Later, as we packed up for the evening, I resolved to do more painting in public places where babes in bikinis hung out. I could even offer to do portraits. The summer in Cornwall was looking up.

When I got home, Mum rushed out into the hall. She had an enormous grin on her face.

'What?' I asked. 'What's happened?'

'You got the job! You got the *job*.'

'The cartooning? How? When?'

'Mr Williams called an hour ago. He said that he was sorry he didn't get back to you sooner but he didn't want to get your hopes up as the cartoons had to go round the building as these things do. Never up to one man or something. But anyway, they were all in agreement. Yours were by far the best so congratulations, Mac. You've got the job. He said to give him a call when you get in. Oh, Mac, I'm so proud of you. You didn't even tell me that you'd sent the cartoons off.'

I felt like someone had blasted a rocket of adrenaline through me. Unbelievable. Me. I'd got the job. *I'd* got the job.

'I've got the job!' I said as I gave Mum a huge hug and we danced round the hall like lunatics.

But that wasn't all. Upstairs on my computer was an e-mail from Emily.

Mac. So sorry about London. Unfinished business, I guess. Michael and I got back together and I realised that actually, it was finished. I want to move forward in my life not backwards so I don't want to go back to him and how we were. I probably need a bit of time on my own for a while — feel what it's like being a singleton and think about what I really want, not charging ahead before I'm ready. But I think I'd like to stay in touch. London's only three hours away so who knows what the future may bring? Love, Emily.

I turned off the computer and went to the window. I'd make my call to Mr Williams then I'd reply to Emily. Or maybe I'd reply to her tomorrow. No hurry.

A feeling of utter contentment came over me. Outside the light was fading and everywhere was still. So quiet. This place is all right, I thought. Another year or two down here will be just fine. Now that I've stopped beating myself up about not being in London, I can start to really enjoy life in Cornwall. Good mates, a summer to look forward to. I'd have some fun. Maybe date a few girls down for their holidays. Already one of the girls we'd met earlier on the beach had given me her number and asked me to call. Maybe I would, maybe I wouldn't.

I felt at peace with my world. For the present, I was happy to be where I was. And then as Emily said, who knows what the future may bring?

After I'd made my call to Mr Williams, I went down to supper. Upstairs on my computer, unbeknown to me until the next day, came another e-mail:

Dearest Mac. Thanks for all your text messages. Congratulations on getting the job. You owe me one! I've been thinking about you a lot these last few days. We've both been too hasty but I know that we have something very special. Call me or I'll call you. Yours, Roz.